Owen B. Maginnis

Roof Framing Made Easy

a practical and easily comprehended system

Owen B. Maginnis

Roof Framing Made Easy
a practical and easily comprehended system

ISBN/EAN: 9783337387303

Printed in Europe, USA, Canada, Australia, Japan

Cover: Foto ©Andreas Hilbeck / pixelio.de

More available books at **www.hansebooks.com**

ROOF FRAMING MADE EASY

OWEN B. MAGINNIS,

Instructor of Drawing in New York Trade School.

Author of "How to Frame a House," "Practical Centring," "How to Join Moldings," etc.

———————

A practical and easily comprehended system of laying out and framing roofs, adapted to modern construction. The methods are made clear and intelligible by 76 engravings with extensive explanatory text.

OWEN B. MAGINNIS, NEW YORK.
1896.

CONTENTS.

———

PREFACE.

I N placing this little work before the student of Architecture or Building Construction, I would state that it is not intended for those
uneducated but for those who, desirous of becoming proficient in the
higher principles of construction, wish to study and apply the best
methods in actual daily practice. With the assurance to the student,
that he will find the contents, if *studied*, will return him full remuneration
by his becoming more valuable on account of his increased knowledge, I
send it forth confidently. The cardboard models will prove the accuracy
of the methods described. The articles being originally published in
The Carpenter, are now issued edited and revised.

The entire work is dedicated to my wife, by whose aid and encour-
agement I have been enabled to persevere and succeed in technical
principles.

THE AUTHOR.

New York City, 1896.

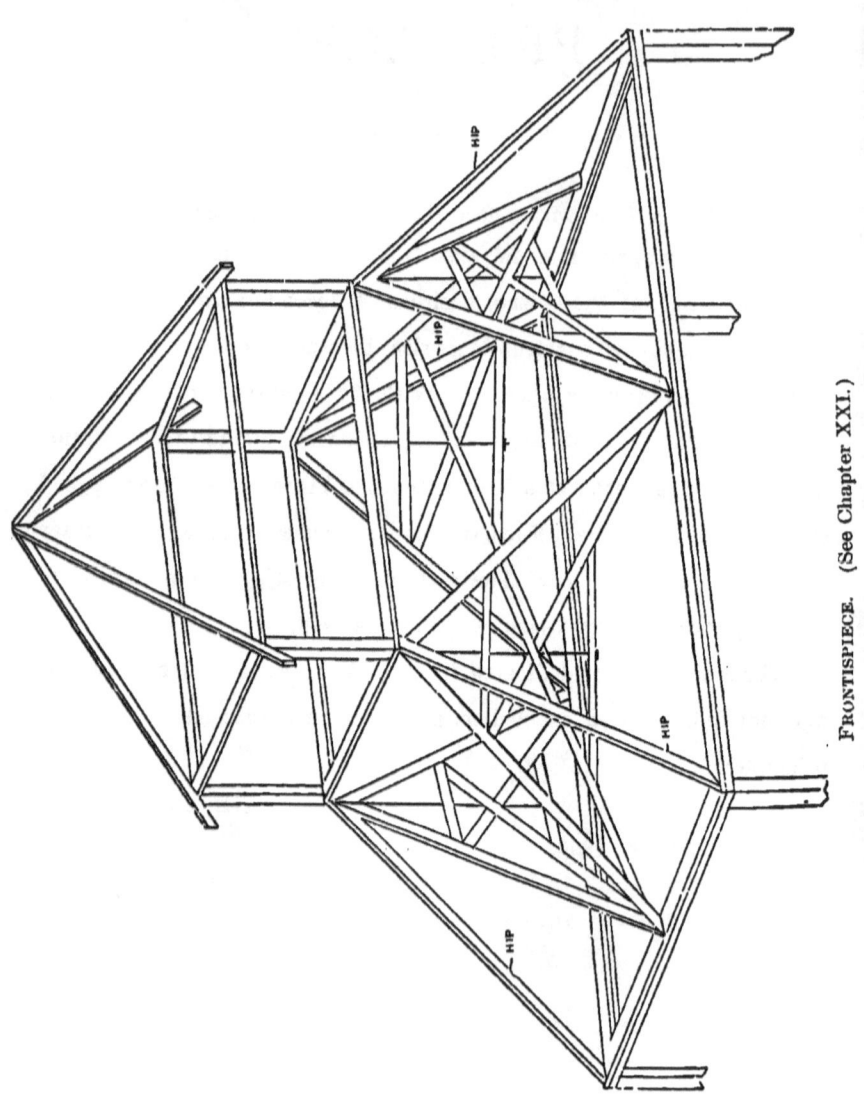

FRONTISPIECE.   (See Chapter XXI.)

ROOF FRAMING MADE EASY.

CHAPTER I.

The Principle of the Roof and General Directions.

WITH a view of explaining the principle of the truss and its practical application in the construction of roofs and bridges, I have commenced with this chapter.

Let A B and A C be two rafters resting together at the ridge or point, as A. Even by their own weight, these two rafters would have a tendency to slip at the points B and C, and to sink at A. If a tie rod or beam be stretched from B to C, and the rafters, A B and B C, be made stiff or rigid, and the tie, B C, not liable to stretch, then A will be made a fixed point. This is the ordinary roof of two rafters in which the tie, B C, is the attic floor beams, and which form may be used for houses of small span.

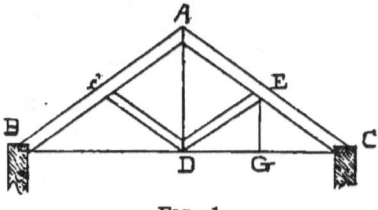

FIG. 1.

When the span is wide, so wide in fact that the tie, B C, being unsupported in the centre, tends to sag by reason of its length, then the conditions of stability are injured. Now if from the point or peak A a string or tie be let down and attached to the middle of B C, as D, it will then be impossible for B C to bend or sag down, as long as A B and B C are the same length. D will be also like a stationary point if the suspension on tie A D be of iron or wood and not stretch. But the span may be increased, or the size of the rafters A B and A C diminished until the rafters tend to sag, and to prevent this, "struts," as D E and D F, are set in, reaching from the stationary point D to the middle of each rafter, or to the centre of its length, as E and

F; thus making E and F stationary points, provided the struts E D and F D remain their full length.

By this means the "truss" or tie up, the point D, and the frame, A B D C, is a trussed frame, or in the term applied in carpentry, a "truss." Similarly, if D C be long its centre can be suspended from the fixed point E by a suspension rod, as E G.

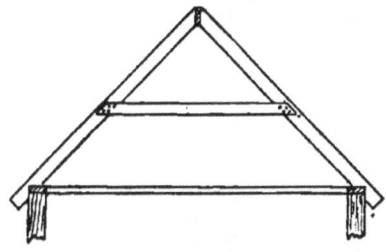

FIG. 2.

In every truss there are two principal strains exerted on the pieces. These are termed *Compression* and *Tension*. For this simple truss the rafters A B and A C are in *Compression*, or being pushed together. A D and B C are extended, or in *Tension*. Those which are in tension can either be made of wood (as wood is very little liable to stretch) or of wrought iron rods, but never of ropes, or any material likely to stretch.

From the above, the student will understand that: the rafters, by their not being subject to compression or crushing, and the tie rod or beam, not being liable to stretch, or, in better words, subject to tension, and the suspension rod complete the truss, thus preventing the sagging of the centre of the tie beam.

In modern roof construction, engineers, as a rule, use timber for rafters and struts and iron for tie and suspension rods; these materials being light and easily put together; and I am sure many readers will meet roofs of this class.

In the ordinary form of house roof shown at Fig. 2, the rafters are in *compression*, the ties, or attic floor beams,

in *tension*, and the col-
lar beam is in compres-
sion, as it takes the place
of the struts, yet gives
the head room.

GENERAL DIRECTIONS.

Roofs should be laid
out to a scale on a large
sheet of detail paper
or on a drawing-board,
using a lead pencil and
two-foot rule or steel
square. The writer gen-
erally uses either 3 inch
or 1½ inch scale; if pos-
sible, as it sometimes is
on small work, full size.

The reason these are
the best working scales
is because the *three inch
scale* works as follows:

3   inches = 1 foot
1½   "   = 6 inches
1   "   = 4   "
½   "   = 2   "
¼   "   = 1   "
⅛   "   = ½   "
1/16 "   = ¼   "
1/32 "   = ⅛   "

The *one and a half*
inch scale is similar but
the divisions are not so
handy. For instance:

1½ inches = 1 foot
¾   "   = 6 inches
½   "   = 4   "
¼   "   = 2   "
⅛   "   = 1   "
1/16 "   = ½   "
1/32 "   = ¼   "

The above two scales
are the best working
scales with the excep-
tion of the half size
proposition which is very
simple and easily applied
thus :

6   inches = 1 foot
5   "   = 10 inches
4   "   = 8   "
3   "   = 6   "
2   "   = 4   "
1   "   = 2   "
½   "   = 1   "
¼   "   = ½   "
⅛   "   = ¼   "
1/16 "   = ⅛   "
1/32 "   = 1/16 "

The foregoing scales
are the best for mechan-
ics, either foremen or at
the works. The full
size laying out is best

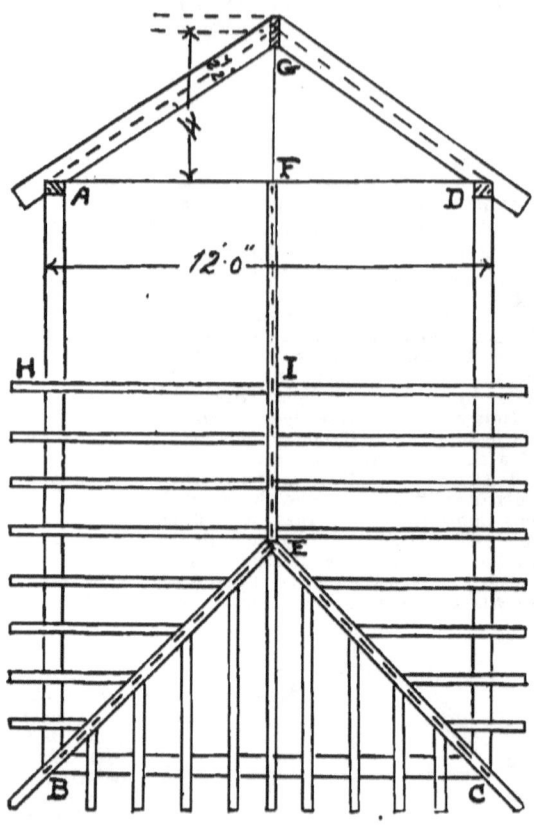

FIG. 3—PLAN OF RAFTERS.

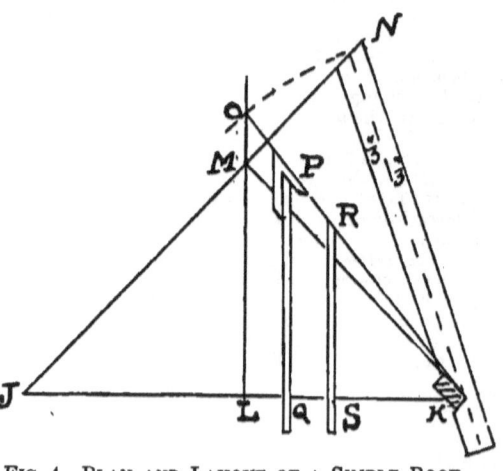

FIG. 4—PLAN AND LAYOUT OF A SIMPLE ROOF.

when possible. Whether the work is laid out to scale or full size, the exact measurements should always be marked in plain figures on every piece.

The figures on the steel square for marking cuts may be used if desired, by placing the square on the scale drawing and noting the figures on the blade and tongue.

CHAPTER II.

LAYING OUT AND FRAMING A SIMPLE ROOF.

LET A, B, C. D, Fig. 3, be the plan of the wall plates. A D a gabled end, and B C a hipped end of the building. The roof is 12 feet wide

inch rafter as shown on the top of Fig. 3, deduct half the thickness of the ridge, half inch, from each rafter peak, cut also notch out for the cut on the plate. All the rafters from F to E will be framed thus:

For the hip rafters, take the distance B; C, and transfer it to J. K, divide it into two parts 6 feet at L, and square up as L. M, O. Join M, J, and M, K. Produce J, M, to N, (dotted line) and join N, K. N, K, will be the centre line length of the hip, and the width may now be set off on each side of it in the manner shown in the diagram.

With K as centre and K, N as radius. strike the arc N, O. cutting L, M extended in O. On L, K lay off the jack rafters as Q. P, S, R, etc. ; equally spaced

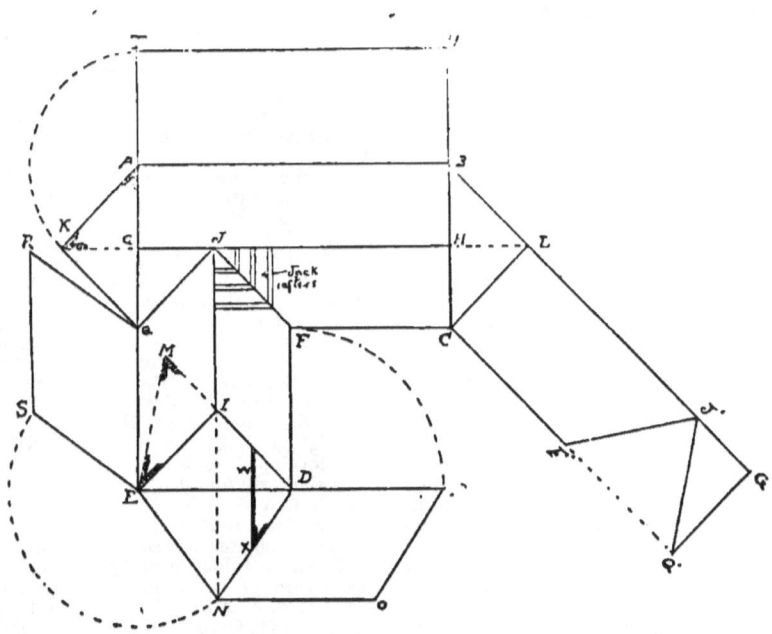

FIG. 5.

to the outside faces of the wall. and the rise or *pitch* 4 feet or one-third the span. The dotted lines denote centre lines.

To lay out the gable end 'produce the center line of the ridge E, I. F to G, and from F measure up 4 feet, join G, A and G, D. Now set off on each side of the dotted line shown, the width of the rafter 2 inches on each side for a 4 inch rafter, and 3 inches on each side for a 6

and square to the wall plate. The exact lengths of the jacks will be to the line O, P, R. K, and their side bevel will be as P. The bottom notch will of course be as at A or D; K shows the bottom notch for the hip rafters and N the peak cut or plumb cut. Great care should be taken to have the lines as accurate as possible, so measurements will be exact.

CHAPTER III.

HIP AND VALLEY ROOFS.

THE next roof which I produce is one of the hip and valley class, or a main rectangular building, with an L or addition. A, B, C, F, D, is the plan of the building and the outside line of the wall plates. The roof is of half pitch or square pitch as some mechanics call it, which means that the height of the roof is equal to half the width of the house. The house has two gables, one on each end of the main part with a hip on the L, and the intersection of the L roof with the main roof produces two valleys. E, I, D, is the plan of the hip and E, J, D, is the elevation of it shown on the elevation Fig. 6, where the general view of the constructed roof is shown. Q, J, and J, F, are the valleys on the plan.

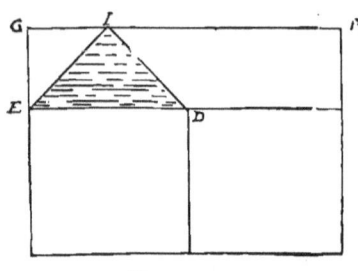

$\mathcal{E}$ LEVATION.

FIG. 6.

In framing this roof the simplest way is as follows:

To obtain lengths and bevels of the common rafter, produce the ridge line G, J, H, to L and K. Join A, K, and K, Q; also B, L, and L, C. A, K, will be the neat length of the common rafter, if no ridge board is inserted; but if there be a ridge board, half its thickness must be sawn off the length on the bevel. K is the bevel for the top or peak cut and A, the bevel for the cut on the plate. Any ordinary mind will see the simplicity of this method.

For the hip rafters which will stand over the seats E, I. and D, I, produce the line D, I, to M, and set off on it the height of the pitch I, M, equal to K, G. Join M, E; M, E, will be the exact length of the hip rafter required, and the bevel at M, will fit the top cut, and that at E, the plate cut. In regard to the cuts for the jack rafters. which run up the hips and valleys. it might be said that the top cuts against the ridges for the rafters which run up the valleys have the *top cut* the same as the com-

mon rafter top cut. The bottom one which nails against, can be readily determined by the following simple method: Produce the ridge line J, I, to N, and make D, N, and N, E, equal to M, E, the length of the hip, W, is the jack on its seat or as it will appear in position. X, is the exact length of it from the plate line to the hip, and the bevel at X, will be the exact bevel for all jacks both on hips and valleys, being reversed for different sides, right and left hand.

The plumb cut of the jacks will be half pitch, or on the steel square, 12 and 12.

In order to prove the exactness of this method of laying out such a roof, we will proceed to develop its planes or sides.

As to the rectangular plane, A, B, G, H, take a pair of compasses with a pencil point, and with A, as centre, and with A, K, radius, describe the arc K, I; draw I, U, parellel to A, B, produce G, A, to I. and H, B, to U, this will give A, B, U, I, the exact covering of A, G, H, B, on the pitch C, K; A, K, being the length of the common rafter with its necessary bevels.

For the plane J, H, C, F, produce B, L to G', and draw C, F, Q, parallel to B, L, J, G'. Make L. J, G'. equal to H, J, G. C, F, equal to C, F, also F', Q', equal to Q, F, make J, F, and J, Q, equal to M, E. which will complete the plane and surface to cover G, J, H, C, F. Q, on the plan.

For the plane J, F, D, I, take D, as centre, with D, F'. radius, and describe the quarter circle F, P. Produce E, D, to P, and through P draw P, O, parallel to D, N, also through N draw N, O, parallel to D, P. D, N, O, P, will be the developed covering, and Q, R, S, E, is similarly found.

B, L, C, and A, K, Q. are the gables.

Now if this roof be laid out on a piece of thin wood or stiff Bristol board the roof can be folded over by cutting entirely through the following lines: Cut from K to A. A to I. I to U, U to B, B to L, L to G', Q' to J', J' to F', F to C. C to F, F to D, D to P, P to O, O to N, N to E, E to S. S to R, and R to Q. Also make a slit half way through the thickness of the board, from Q to A, A to B, B to C. C to L, D to N, D to E, and E to Q. By folding the sides or planes over, the exact roof will be seen, thereby proving the method.

The many apparently complex roofs which are nowadays placed on frame buildings are apt to discourage those young mechanics who are ambitious, so in order to simplify and bring them within the grasp of all I have now adopted a plan of roof of somewhat un-usual form.

At Fig. 7 the plan is A B C D E F G H I J L and K, being the plan of a small frame house costing about $2,000. Fig. 8 is an end view or gable elevation show-ing the pitch is of the common rafters which we will assume to be full pitch, or 12 inches rise and 12 inches run on the steel square. A B is the top line of the plate across the bay, or across the widest part of the house. A K is the span across the main walls and E J the rise or pitch; therefore A J will be the length of the common rafters on the plan Fig 7, that will be set on the plate A K from N to O on the ridge. A G, Fig. 8, is the span across the narrowest part of the house or from A to B, Fig. 7, and E M is the rise or pitch, con-sequently A M will be the length of the short common rafters and the bevels will be as repre-sented at J M and A.

Now to find the lengths of the hips and valleys and bay window rafters, refer to Fig. 7, and com-mencing at the near val-ley C M square up the line M R, make it equal to E M on Fig. 7 and join C R. C R will be the length of the valley with top and bottom bevels as shown. On the seat of the hips N D, square up the rise N T equal to E J, Fig. 7, and join D T for length of hip, with top and plate bevels as at D and T. It will be noticed that these rafters are parallel on the lay-out because their seats are parallel. therefore they must be correct; the val-ley rafter L Q to stand over L P is determined in like manner also the hip S K to stand over O K.

As I have previously shown several ways to obtain the lengths of jack raft-ers on half pitch roofs I will not repeat this simple method here but go on and give layout of bay window timbers.

Referring again to the engraving Fig. 8 we find that the plate line of the bay

C H D is higher or raised up 4 feet above the level of the plate line of the princi-pal or main walls as A G B; to find lengths of rafters we go back again to Fig. 7. Here on the seat of the hip E U we proceed to square up the rise U V and join E V, which will be the length of the hip U V, being equal to the rise

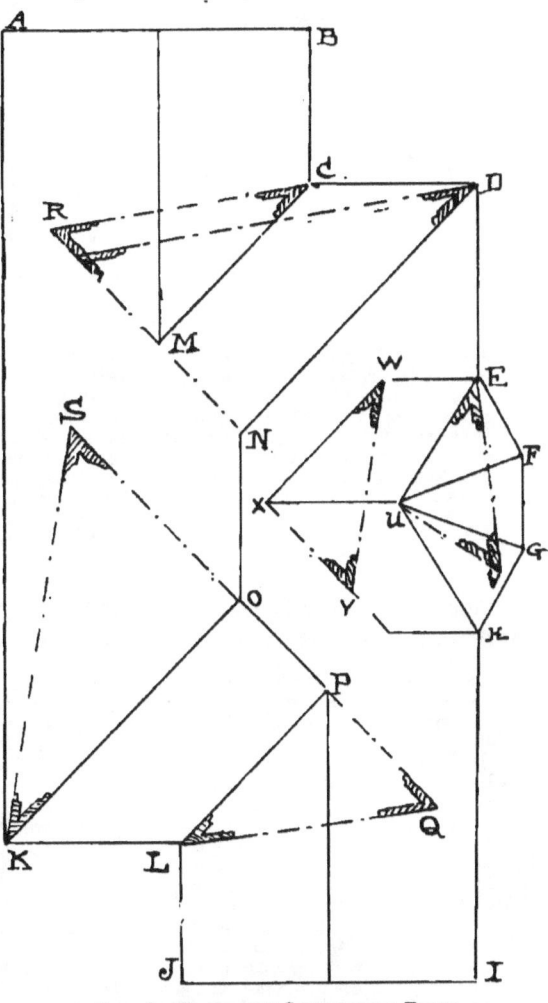

FIG. 7—PLAN AND LAYOUT OF ROOF.

C J, Fig. 8. There will be four hips this length to stand over E U, F U, G U, and H U, on the seat of the W X. Square up the rise X Y and join W Y for length of valley. There will be two needed, one for each side. Jacks can be found as before described. Regarding the jack rafters reaching from the valleys over W X to the hips D N and O P, I might state that the bottom and top cuts will be alike up to the points N and O where the hips join the ridge N O. Against it they will be a square cut on top edge with the down cut as at J Fig. 7.

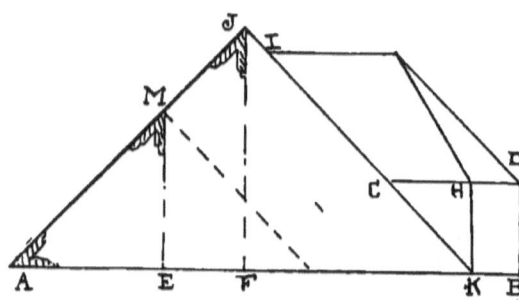

FIG. 8—PROJECTION OF ROOF.

When calculating the timbers or laying out roofs of this description, too much care cannot be bestowed in watching the exact number of rafters required, the right and left hand cuts of the bevels on the jacks, etc., and the exactitude of framing to the neat lengths required so as to prevent mistakes or recutting.

CHAPTER IV.

ROOFS OF IRREGULAR PLAN.

THIS chapter embraces a roof of another and rather uncommon plan, and one which will be interesting to work out. It is a form of roof which sometimes occurs and will prove useful.

A, B, C, D, Fig. 9, is the plan, and it will be noticed that the side walls are not parallel, or at equal distance apart from end to end, but spread or widen out from A to B, and from C to D, or B, D, is longer than A, C. Similarly A, B, is longer than C, D, and not parallel to C, D. For this reason coupled with the necessity of keeping the ridge level on both sides a deck is formed on the top, or more properly two ridges are needed, one for each side, and parallel to each wall plate; these are shown as E, F, and E, G.

The seats of the hips as A, E. C, E, B, F, and D, G, are found by bisecting each of the separate angles on the plan, which can be done by taking any two points equidistant from the apex of the angle as A. and striking intersecting arcs. (As every student knows how to

do this I will not illustrate it here.) This process will give the seats of the hips as shown and lettered, with the addition of a short piece of ridge F, G.

To find the lengths and bevels of the rafters, proceed as follows:—For the common rafters to range from U, E, to V, F, on the one side, and from E, W, to G, X, on the other side; raise up the pitch G, P. Square out from G to X, and join P, X which joining line will be the exact length of the common rafter from outer edge of plate to centre line of ridge. To obtain length of hip rafters square up from each point at the peaks, as E, H; F, I. on one side. Make E, H, and F, I, each equal to G, P; A, H, and B, I, will be the lengths of the hip rafters, which will rise over A· E, and B, F. The hip rafters which will be set up over the seats, C, E, and D, G, are determined in a similar manner. The top and bottom bevels delineated at the peaks and bottoms are the top and bottom cuts of each, and it will be noticed that no two bevels are alike, so that each rafter must be carefully laid out and marked for each particular corner. There will be four hips of different lengths and with different bevels, so they must be properly framed. In regard to the jack rafters they are shown on the right side spaced out on the wall plate from X to D, against the hip, G, D. Their top down bevel or plumb cut will be the same as that at P, and that at R will be the side bevel. Similarly with those from D to M, the plumb cut will be the same as P, but the bevel will be that at O.

In order to develop the planes of this roof, commence by drawing E. U, S, from E, through W, at right angles to E. F, or A. B; also draw F, V, T, parallel to E. U, S. Make A, S, equal to A, H, by taking A as center with radius A. H, and striking the arc H, S. Through S, draw S, T, parallel to A, B. If a center be taken at B, and an arc struck as I. T, N, it will be found that the arc will pass through T. or F, V, produced at T. The surface A. S, T, B, will cover the plan. A, E, F, B. on the pitch E, H.

Draw E, J. square to A, C, and produce to K. Sweep H, S, to K, and join A, K, and K, C. A, K. C, will be the covering plane which will cover over A, E, C, on plan. For the plane of A, E, G,

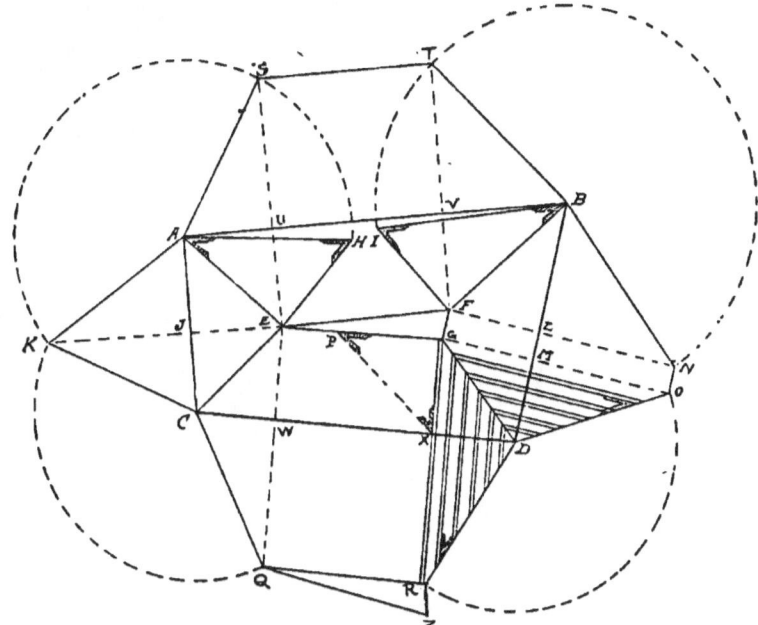

FIG. 9.

D, draw E, W, square to E, G, and produce to Q. With C as centre and C, K, as radius, strike the arc K. Q; draw Q. R, parallel to C, D. Join C, Q, which will be the centre of the hip rafter on this side. Draw G, X, square to C, D, and produce to R; join R, D, C:Q, R, D. will be the covering plane which will cover over C, E, G, D, on the pitch G, P.

Now draw G, M, and F. L, square to B, D, and produce them to N and O.

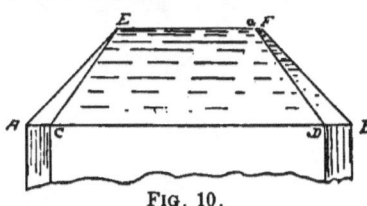

FIG. 10.

With D, as centre and D, R, as radius describe the arc R, O, also the T. N. Join N, O, B; N, O, D, will be the covering of the plan B, F. G, D, on the pitch G, P. Q, R, Y, Z, will be the covering or deck, being the same size or area as E, F, G.

At Fig. 10 will be seen the elevation, or as it will appear when framed, raised and covered.

A model can be made of this roof by cutting out the entire outside line of the covering and making a slit from A to B, from B to D, from D to C, from C to A, also from Q to R, which being folded up will show the completed roof with the rafters, cuts and bevels in position.

CHAPTER V.

SQUARE PYRAMIDAL ROOFS.

ROOF framing is a study well worthy the attention of every student of building construction. The roof illustrated and described in this chapter is one which occurs on many cottages and houses now-a-days. It is one of a kind of tower roofs on a square plan or as they are sometimes termed "Pyramidal roofs." A, C, D, F, Fig. 11, is the projection of the roof completed. A, C, D, B, Fig. 12, the plan cf the roof on the plates; AE, CE. DE and BE, being the hips which form the shape of the roof or seats over AF, CF, DF, on Fig. 11, stand. The fourth hip over BE, cannot be seen on the projection, Fig. 11.

In order to find the length of the hips, produce the line E, B. indefinitely. Now set off, measuring from E, the height of the peak to F, Fig. 11. Join

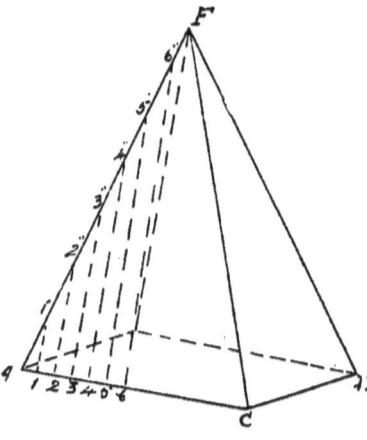

Fig. 11.

AF, Fig. 12, which will be the exact length of either of the four hips. In framing this roof it is best to let two op-

posite hips as BE, and EC, on the same line abut against each other at the peak, and to cut off their thickness from the other two top or peak cuts, thus: If BE, and EC. be each 2 inches thick then 1 inch will be cut off the peak cuts of AE, and DE which rest against them at E. This is done in the same manner, as every top cut of a rafter resting against a ridge must have half the thickness of the ridge cut from each rafter. The bevel at F, Fig. 12, is the bevel of all four top cuts and that at A, the bevel for the cuts on the plate.

Concerning the jack rafters, the best way to determine their length is to set them off the plate as from A to C, Fig. 12, then to draw a line as H, E, G, through E, parallel to AC, or BD. With A, as centre and AF, as radius describe the arc FG, cutting the H, E, G, at G. Join G, A, and G, B. The triangle, or more properly speaking, the triangular surface G, A, B, will be the exact covering surface of the roof plane A, E, B.

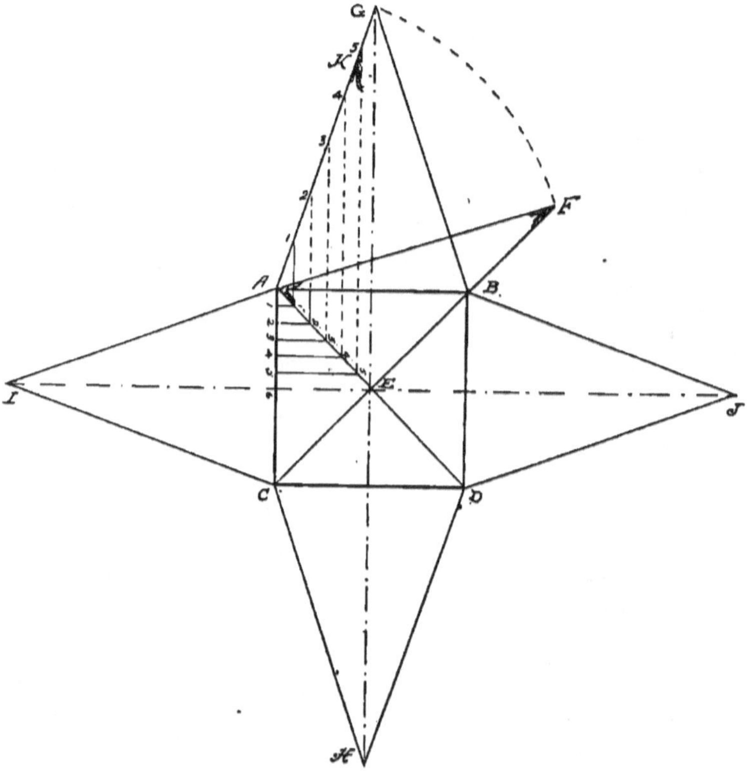

Fig. 12.

From where the jack rafters come against the hip AE, draw lines parallel to E, G, and square to A, B, cutting A G, as shown. The lines reaching from the plan line A, B, to A, G, will be the exact jack rafters and the bevel at K, will be the side cut against the hip, with the bevel at F, as the vertical cut, and that at K, the bottom or plate cut.

The development of the covering for the remaining three planes of the roof is found by drawing the line I, J, through E, parallel to A, B, or C, D; then with B, as centre and B, G, as radius intersecting E, J at J, and joining J, B and J, D; a similar process can be gone through to determine the points H. and I, thus obtaining the four convexing planes.

To prove the accuracy of this and the two previous roof problems before described, or in fact any roof problem, the plan should invariably be laid out to a scale, say $1\frac{1}{4}$ inches to 1 foot. On a sheet of cardboard $\frac{1}{4}$ inch scale will do if the roof be very large, then to make a cardboard model. Here this can be done and when the lines have been laid down, as just described, the entire model may be made as follows:—With a sharp pocketknife cut clean through the cardboard from A to G, from G to B, from B to J, from J to D, from D to H, from H to C, from C to I, and from I to A. Next make a slit halfway through the cardboard from A to B, from B to D, from D to C, and from C to A. Proceed to fold the planes over the seats till they all join at the edges, thereby making a completed cardboard roof resembling Fig. 11 with the jacks and bevels in position, and with all the cuts fitting as they ought to.

CHAPTER VI.

To Frame a Pentagonal Roof.

SOME time since the writer was required to lay out a pentagonal or five-sided band stand which had a slate roof terminating in a wooden finial at the apex. As this roof is of a form rarely met with in building construction, I introduce it here, being under the impression that readers might perhaps have occasion to use the lines for such a roof. However, as there are pavilions, pagodas or summer houses built on this plan, I think it wise to describe it as the knowledge is easily carried and may prove useful.

Fig. 13 illustrates the simplest and most accurate method of, striking out a *pentagon*, or five-sided figure, one side being given. For example, if the length of one plate line as E D, Fig. 14, be drawn to a scale on any plan, the carpenter can very readily lay out his pentagon full size or half size, as follows:—Let C E, Fig. 13, be any line equal to the line E D, Fig. 14. Divide C E, into two parts at G, and produce C G E. Make E J, equal to C E, and with E, as centre and radius E C, describe the semi-circle C K L F J. Divide the semi-circle into five equal parts at the points K L F and M. From the point G, square up the line G I. Join E and F, and bisect the joining line E F, at H. From H, square out,

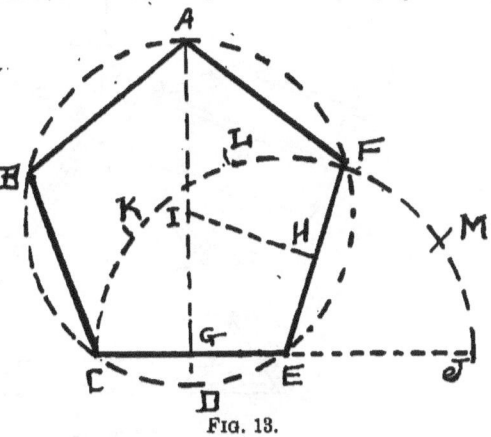

FIG. 13.

cutting the line G I, at I, and with I as centre and F as radius, describe the circle A B C D E F. Set the compasses or a rod to the length C E, or E F, and space off round the circle, also join the points together by lines and complete the *pentagon*, as indicated by the heavy black lines.

In order to lay out the hip and jack rafters for a roof of this description, proceed to Fig. 14, and lay out the outside lines of the plates as A B, B C, C D, and D E, also with the compasses, describe the thickness of the finial or boss, against which the top ends of the five hip rafters rest, also lay out the hip rafters as indicated in the diagram in three lines; the centre one being the line of the *backing*, and those on either side the thickness of the hip. By *backing* is meant *beveling* the top edges of the hip to permit the roof-boards or

sheathing to lie on the solid timber instead of only on the sharp *arris* or edge
of the rafter. The seats of the jack

centre or apex and B. Fig. 14. Square
up from the apex as X, equal in height
to the pitch or rise of the roof. Join B

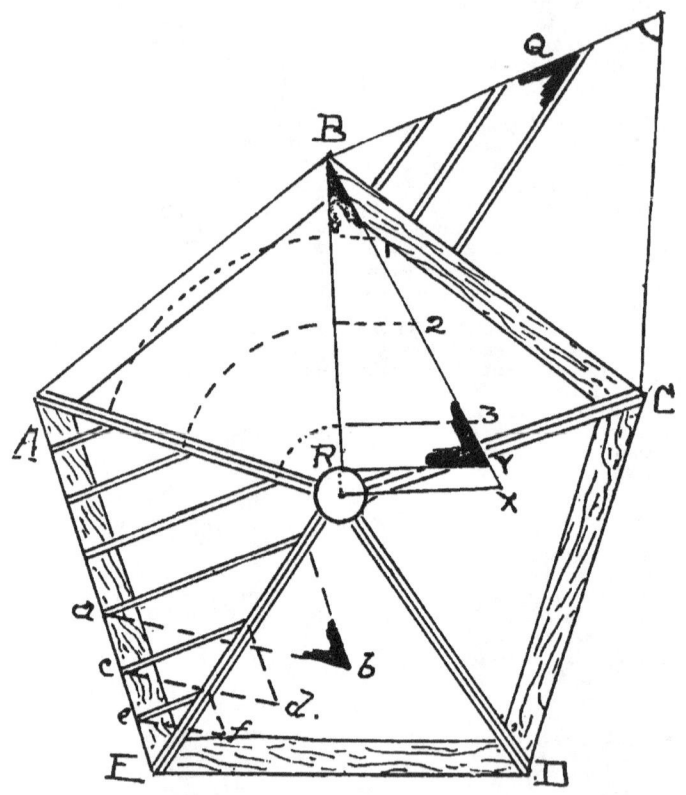

FIG. 14.

rafters may also be laid down as shown.
To find length of hip rafters join the

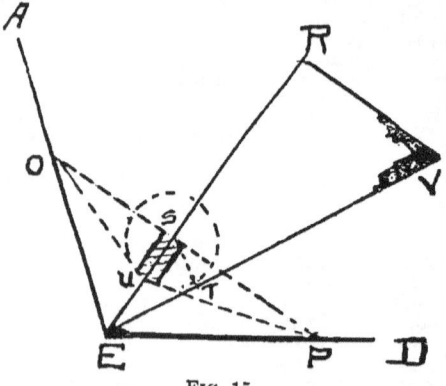

FIG. 15.

and X, to obtain the length of the hip
and its apex and plate cuts, seen in the
diagram. There will, of course,
be five hip rafters this length
required. The length of each
jack rafter may be obtained in a
very simple way by squaring up
from each jack where each rests
against the hip and setting off
each height of each jack, thus
determining the exact length of B
Z C, being the development of the
B R C. The side bevel will be as
Q, which must be reversed for
jack on opposite sides of the hips.
There will be five sets with a
right-hand side bevel and five
sets with a left-hand side bevel.
    Regarding the backing of the
five hip rafters, the first thing to
be done is to find the desired
bevel. This is easily accom

plished by taking any point, as S, Fig. 15, and from S, drawing square to E R, as O P. From S. let fall a line perpendicular to E V, as S T. With S as centre and S T as radius, describe the circle S T U cutting R E, at U. Join U P and U O. O U P, will be the bevel of the backing and a bevel may be set to one side of the rafter.

CHAPTER VII.

HEXAGONAL PYRAMIDAL ROOFS.

READERS will see at Fig. 16 the top and side views of a hexagonal or six-sided roof, or one which has a wall plate running round on six walls as shown above, the dotted lines representing the angle lines of the hexagonal figure. The completed roof with the boarding or tin on will appear as shown on lower sketch.

In order to frame this roof the following system should be used:

At Fig. 16 proceed to lay out on a board or paper to a scale of 1½ or 3 inches to the foot, the plan of the wall plates (on the outside line). *A, B, C. D, E, F ; and join the points of the intersections of the sides, as A D, B E, and C F ; passing through the centre G. This gives the seats of the hip rafters A G, B G, C G, D G, E G and F G ; six in all. To find their exact length, square up from E. G, as G, J. Lay off also to the same scale, the exact height in feet of pitch or rise of the roof from G, to J, and join J, E, which line will be the exact length of the hip rafter as seen in the diagram with the top and bottom bevels necessary for the cuts, these being given at once without any uncertainty.

To find the length of the common rafter, to stand over H, G, set off the pitch G. I, on G, C, equal to G, J, and join H, I, for its length. This rafter is rarely used on roofs of this class, except when they are of large area, as only the jacks are requisite, especially on modern frame houses where they seldom exceed eight feet in width, thus requiring short rafters.

To develop this roof take a pair of compasses, and with E. as centre, and radius E. J. describe the arc J, M L, cutting H, G, produced in L. Join E, L, and D, L, which will give the triangle E, L, D, the covering over the plan E. G, D, on the pitch or rise G, J. Bisect, or rather divide E, F, into two parts at Q. Square up from Q, cutting the arc J. M. L, at M. Join M, E and M, F. The triangle E, M, F,⋮ will lie

over E. G, F. The remaining four triangular developments or coverings can be laid out from the foregoing by making J, O, H, K, R, N, and S, P, equal in length to Q, M, or a simpler method would be to take G, as centre with G, M. as radius and describe short arcs cutting O, K, N. and P, thus giving the exact lengths at one sweep, and insuring their being alike so as to meet at the centre G when folded.

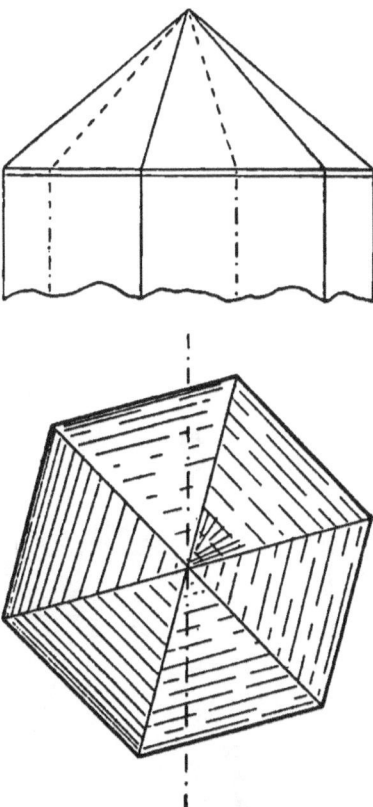

FIG. 16.

The side bevel at K, will make the top cuts on the jack rafters fitting against the hips, the bottom cuts fitting on the plates being the bevel at H.

Almost every mechanic knows how a hexagon or six-sided figure is struck out, still in case there should be even one student who is at sea in regard to it, I repeat the method of doing so here. The diameter or length from angle to angle is usually given, or if not, is easily found by joining the angles as before described. Now to lay out any hexagon, draw any line as F, C, and divide it into two equal parts at G. With G, centre and radius G, F, strike the circle A, B, C, D, E, F. Now take a pair of dividers (sharp points on both legs) and from C, with one point on C, space out the six distances C, B, B, H, A, F, F, E, E, D, and D, C. Draw the lines as shown for the outline of the hexagon.

modern houses, barns, etc. The methods to be followed in this chapter are very simple, so that an ordinary mechanic can easily understand them if he only studies the diagram and text a little.

Supposing A, B, C, D, E, F, G, H, on Fig. 18 to be the plan or plate line of the roof. and O, L. the pitch or rise, it can be laid out as follows: To be more

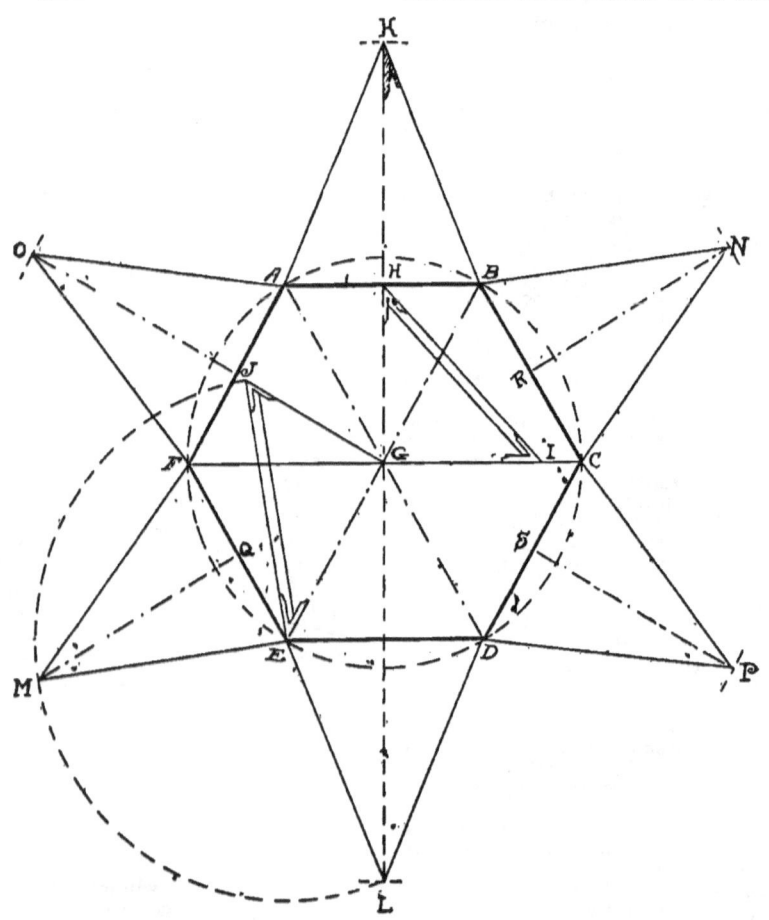

FIG. 17.

CHAPTER VIII.

CONICAL ROOFS.

HAVING treated the usual forms of roofs embracing the hip and valley principles, I will now draw attention to the proper laying out and framing of a roof on a circular tower, as this form occurs very often in

explicit I will take it for granted that a carpenter has a roof to frame with a plan A. B, etc., of 6 feet diameter, or 6 feet from C to G, and 9 feet rise, or from O to L is 9 feet. Proceed to strike the plan A, B, etc., either full size or to scale. It is always better to lay out full size if a floor or drawing-board can be found big enough to do it, but if not, half size or a scale of 3 inches or 1½ inches to the foot may be used.

Having struck the circle, draw centre lines for the rafters A E, B F, C G, and D H, and set off the thickness of the rafters as they show on the plan. Next draw any straight line as J K, the same length as C G; raise up the centre line O L, the height of the pitch, and join L K, which will be the length of the rafters to stand over A I, B I, C I, D I, E I, F I, and G I and the top and bottom cuts will be directly given; as at L and J, L M and L N are the rafters I D and

may be determined by striking out the sweeps shown on the plan, 1 1, 2 2, 3 3, 4 4, and 5 5. It will be noticed that this roof will require 8 circular pieces for each row, or 40 sweeps in all. One pattern will do for each sweep and the remaining 8 needed can be marked from each pattern.

Fig. 19 will convey a better idea of the constructed roof, as this illustration represents each stud, plate, rafter and sweep in its fixed position, with the covering boards nailed on half way round.

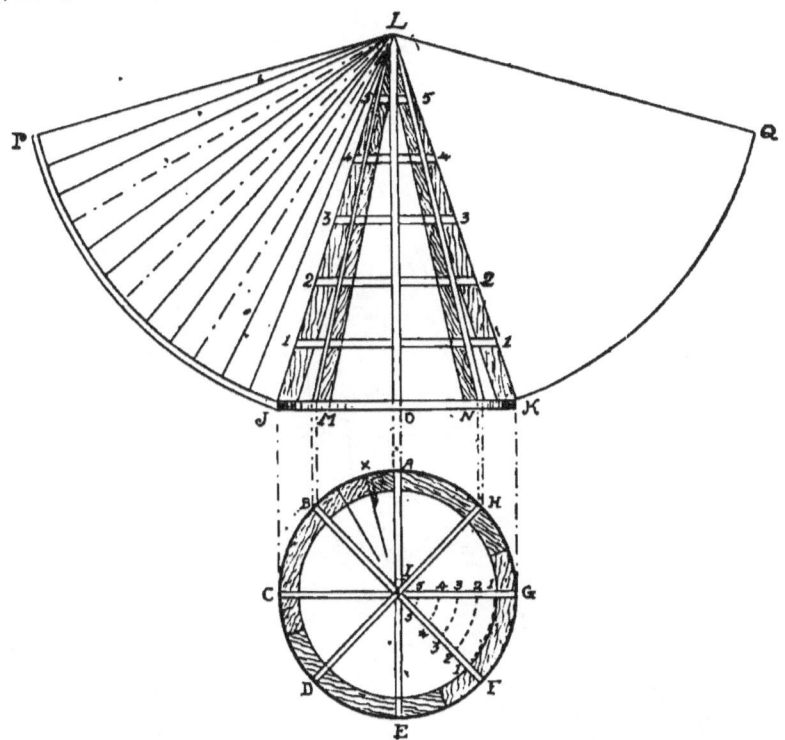

FIG. 18.

I E placed in position and L O is the rafter E I in position. By referring to Fig. 19 the rafters B I, A I and H I will be seen at the rear of the figure.

If the roof is to be boarded vertically, horizontal strips or *sweeps* will require to be sawn out and nailed in, in the manner represented in both Figs. 18 and 19. To do this properly, divide the height from O to L in Fig. 18 and draw the lines representing the sweeps as 1 1, 2 2, 3 3, 4 4, and 5 5. The neat length, and the cuts to fit against the sides of the rafters

In order to find the exact shape and levels for the covering boards. a very simple method is used, thus: Take a pair of compasses, or a trammel rod, and with L as centre, and L P as radius, describe the arcs J P and K Q. Join L P and L Q, now divide the half circle A, B, C, D, E, into 12 equal spaces on J P, with a pair of compasses, and join the division marks on J P with L. This will give 12 tapering boards and the bevel at X on the plan will be the bevel of the jointed edges. As twelve boards

FIG. 19.

will be needed for half the plan, twenty-four will have to be cut out for the other half, so it will be seen that if the sweep or arc J P goes round from A B to E, the sweep K Q will go round H, K, G, etc., to E. The diminishing lines from the point L to the line J P are the inside lines of the joints of the boards shown also in Fig. 19.

In order to prove the rectitude of the foregoing, a model can be made by drawing the roof to scale on cardboard, and then cutting out the figures from L to J, from J to K, and from K to L. Also cut out the figures L P S, and L Q K. Now if L S K be stood up over A, E, B, F, etc., it will be seen to fit over each.

In a similar way the figure L J P will bend around A B C D E with the peak L over the point I and the line J P around A B C D E. In a like manner K Q will bend around A H G F E. and L will lie over I, thus proving the correctness of the methods followed. Care must be taken to allow for the intervening rafters when framing the peak cuts of the rafters.

* * *

CHAPTER IX.

TO FRAME A CONICAL ROOF INTERSECTED BY A PITCHED ROOF.

AS this is a roof which occurs in many cases, especially in railroad work, it will be found both interesting and useful.

Let A E F B V, Fig. 20, be the plan or wall plate of the conical dome, and A D B, the diameter, also D C, the rise or pitch. Join A C, to obtain the lengths of the common rafters which will radiate from the centre C, round the circular plate A E F B V, with the top and bottom bevels as represented at C and A.

On account of the pitched roof C H F, the gable end of which is G I H, with pitch J I, equal in height to D C, intersecting or cutting into the conical dome, there will be a valley rafter. The seat of this valley will be D F. because J I, being equal to C D, the ridge J E, will be the same height as the conical apex or peak D.

To obtain the length of the valley rafter, square up from D, and with D, as centre and D C, as radius, cut off the length D K, equal to D C. Join F K. F K, will be the length of the valley, and as D B, is equal to D F, and the pitches D C. and D K. are equal, therefore the valley will be the same length as common rafter.

To find the lengths of jack rafters, proceed to Fig. 21, and lay out the ridge and valley rafter as before. With F as

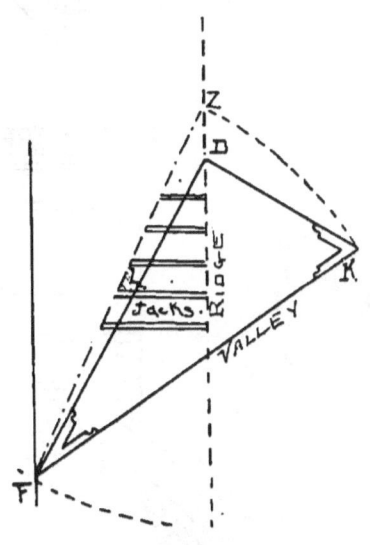

FIG. 21.

centre, and F K, as radius, describe the curve K Z, cutting the ridge at Z. Join F Z. The lengths of the jacks will be as shown on the left side of the ridge.

The final process is to determine the shape of the covering or roof boards which are laid horizontally. To do this take C, Fig. 20, as center. and with equal spaces up the common rafter as P Q R S, strike the parallel curves P T, Q U, R V, and S W. The exact length of the boards is found by dividing F B into five equal parts and setting them off on B X. Join C X, to determine the length of all to the apex. A very successful cardboard model can be made of this roof.

* * *

CHAPTER X.

OCTAGONAL ROOFS.

AT Fig. 22, A B C D E F G H is the plan of the octagonal roof. I is the centre or peak. A I, B I, etc., are the seats of the hips. L J is the length of the common rafters. B K the exact length of the hip rafters.

To find side bevel of hips, produce N I to M, and make B M equal to B K; join M B and M A. The bevel at M will be the side bevel across the top edges of the rafters, and the bevel shown inside

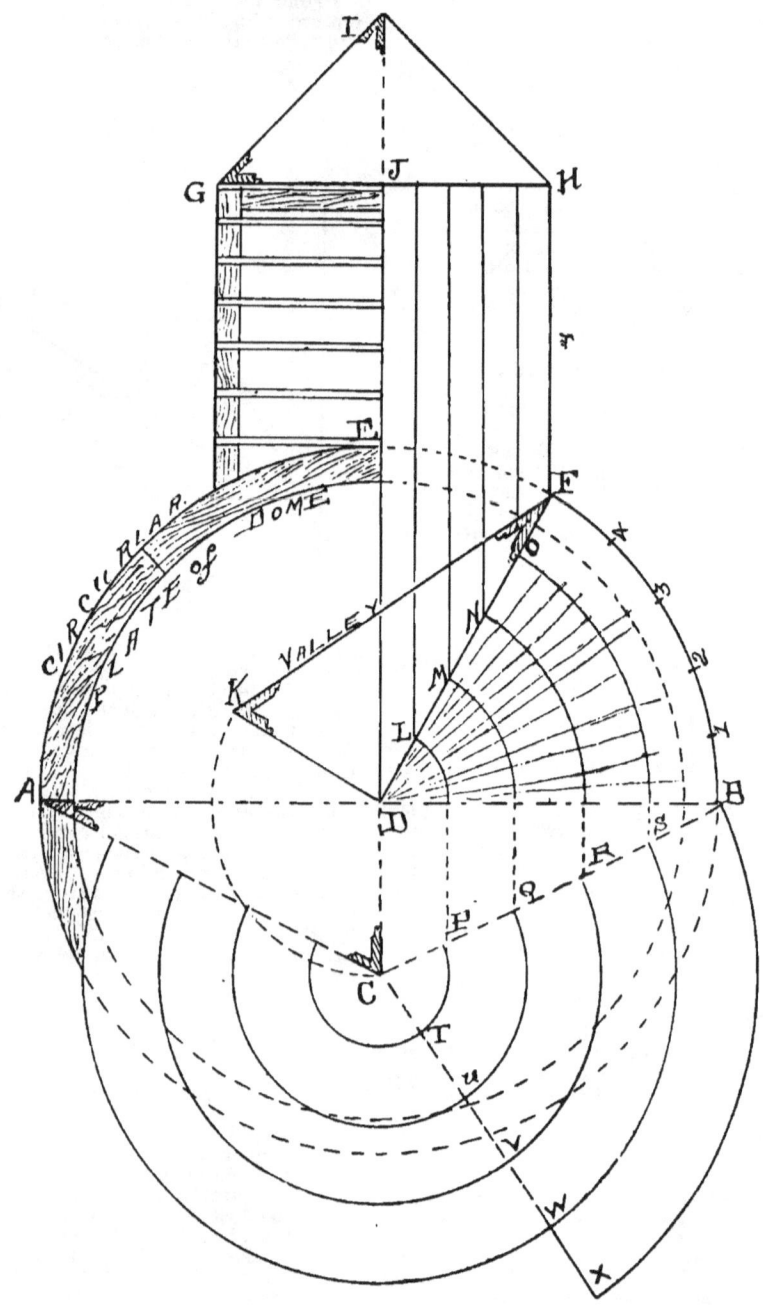

FIG. 20—LAYING OUT OF ROOF.

the hips will be the bevel across the top edges of the jacks, right and left hand.

Proceed to Fig. 23, and to obtain side bevel of octagon hip rafters, on B D,

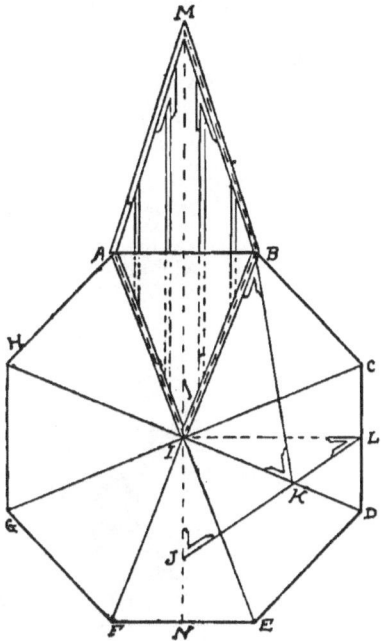

FIG. 22.

the seat of the hip, raise up the pitch D E, join E B for length of hip. To obtain side bevel of jacks, take B as centre and B E as radius, describe arc E F and

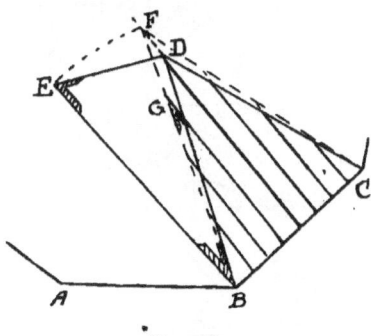

FIG. 23.

join F and B. Produce line of jacks to meet B F, and the bevel at G is the side bevel across top of jacks, applied right and left, and on right and left sides of hip.

CHAPTER XI.

FRAMING AN OCTAGONAL ROOF OF GOTHIC SECTION.

AS all are interested in unusual problems in carpentry, I have pleasure in laying before them in this chapter one which I solved and which is worth studying out. It was erected on a cupola of a large institution building in the city of New York, and is to-day standing complete according to the architect's design.

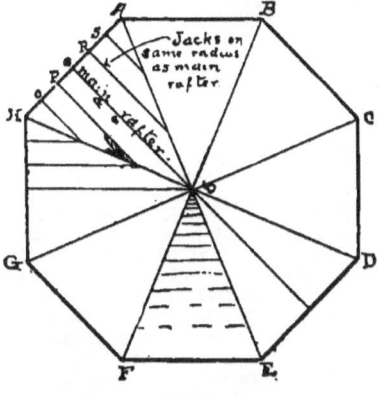

FIG. 24.

A, B, C, D, E, F, G, H, Fig. 24, was the plan of the cupola or lantern, eight-sided in shape as will be seen. Its elevation was as represented in Fig. 25, and its section was a gothic of the equilateral form, as G 6, D 6, Fig. 25, F 6, and E 6, were the hip lines of the octagonal plan to stand over on Fig. 24, the seats F 6, and E 6. The radius of the gothic was as shown on the elevation, and from this we will proceed to lay out the roof and and get the curves for the timbers.

From the points T, U, V, W, X, draw lines square to Q 6', as IL, UM, VN, WI, X. From the space points on the line QZ, make the dotted lines equal in length individually to TL, UM, VN, WI, X; and draw through the points the curve Z, Y, G. Produce NS, and WR to Y and Y', and the lines SY' and RY will denote the curved jack rafters. The bevel at Y, is that which will fit against the side of the hip rafter as the development G, Z, Q, will fold and stand over the G 6', Q. The curve of the jacks will be the same as G 6, Fig. 24, and struck from the same radius. This will be readily understood by an examination of the diagram, Fig. 26. The bevel A 6, Fig. 25, will be the plumb cut of the jack rafters.

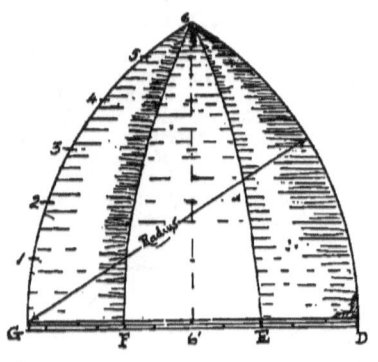

FIG. 25.

Also, draw level lines from the points 1, 2, 3, 4, 5, on 6', 6, cutting the plumb lines from G', 6', at the points 1', 2', 3', 4', 5', 6'. Draw the curve G 1, etc., through these points and this curve will be the exact shape of the hip rafter required to stand over the eight seats seen on Fig. 24.

For the jacks divide the plate G F. Fig. 26, into six equal parts and draw lines square to the plate for the seats of the jacks, as will be seen from A to H, Fig. 24. These will join with the lines 2 U, 4 W, at the points U and W on the line G' 6'. Produce them indefinitely outside G', F'. Now take the divisions G' 7', Fig. 24, and set them off on the line Q Z, Fig. 26, and draw lines square to Q Z.

In order to find the length and curve of the hip rafters which will stand over the seats on Fig. 24, A 6, B 6, C 6. D 6, E 6, F 6, G 6, H6, proceed as follows: Take any octagonal triangle as G 6 F, Fig. 24, and lay it off as G' 6' F', Fig. 26. G 6, being a level line. From 6' raise up a plumb line as 6', 6. Next divide the gothic sweep on Fig. 24, G 6, into six equal parts, as 1, 2, 3, 4. 5, 6, and carry these over to the centre line 6', 6, by horizontal or level lines as indicated. Transfer these to 6', 6, Fig. 26. Next divide the line G' 6', into six equal parts, as T, U, V, W, X, and from the points of division raise up plumb lines.

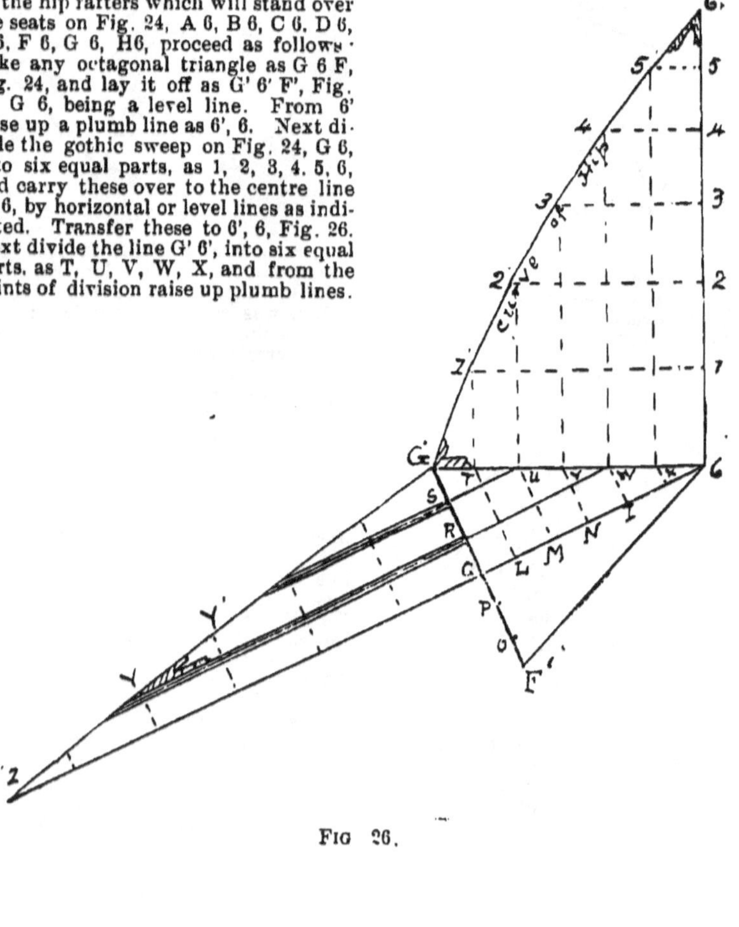

FIG 26.

CHAPTER XII.

FRAMING AN OCTAGONAL MOLDED ROOF.

THE molded roof which I propose to treat in this chapter is one which may not be familiar to readers and may seem difficult to lay out. Various methods have been put forward

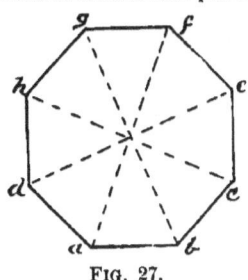

FIG. 27.

for the purpose of getting the exact cuts, etc., for these roofs, but there have

been none so far sufficiently intelligible to apply practically. I have, therefore, worked out one of the most usual forms for the benefit of the trade at large.

The first roof is a regular "ogee" molded tower roof on an octagonal or eight-sided plan. or, in other words. the plate is eight-sided, as represented at

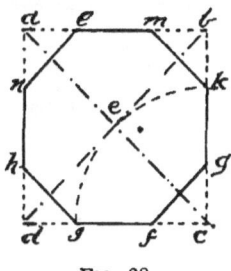

FIG. 28.

Fig. 29, where the plan of the rafters is denoted, including both hips and jacks.

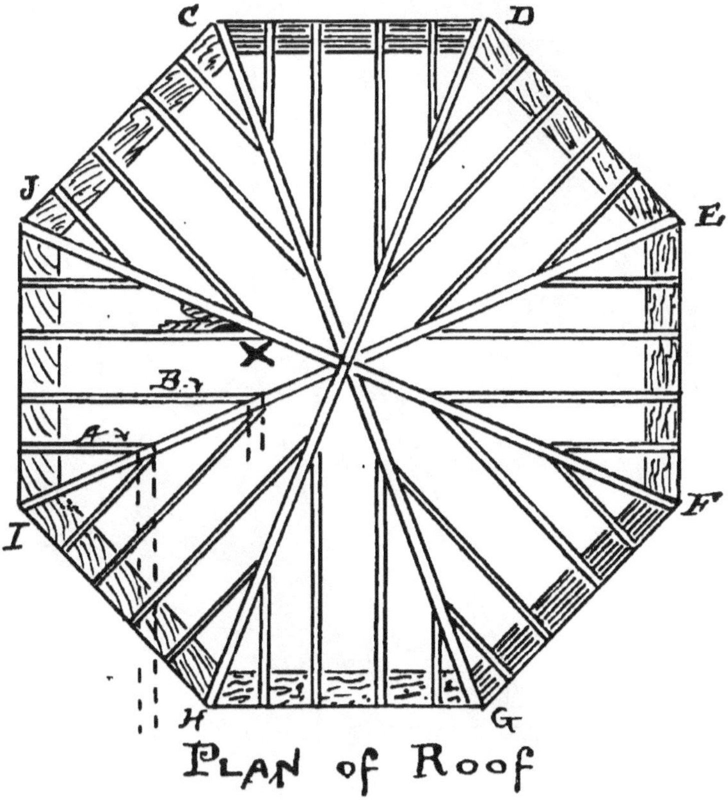

PLAN of Roof

FIG. 29.

C, D, E, F, G, H, I and J is the eight-sided plate, and eight sides have a molded plane terminating in a point at L, shown in the layout, Fig. 30.

As there may perhaps be some readers who are not entirely familiar with the proper ways of making an eight-sided figure or octagon, I will explain this here. Let a, b, Fig. 27, be one side of the octagon, say 4 feet long, it is required to construct the full octagon 8 feet 6 inches wide. To do this: With the steel square or bevel, draw a-d and

b-c on a miter, and make each 4 feet long; then from c and d, draw c, e and d, h, square to a, b. Next from e and h, draw e, f and h, g, on a miter of 45 degrees, and make each 4 feet long; join g and f, to complete the figure. This alone is one way to do it, and a very simple one. Fig. 28 shows another way: Let a d, d c and c b be any square, say 8 feet 6 inches wide. Draw the diagonals from corner to corner, as a c and b d, cutting in e. Now with the compasses set to e c mark the sides at J and

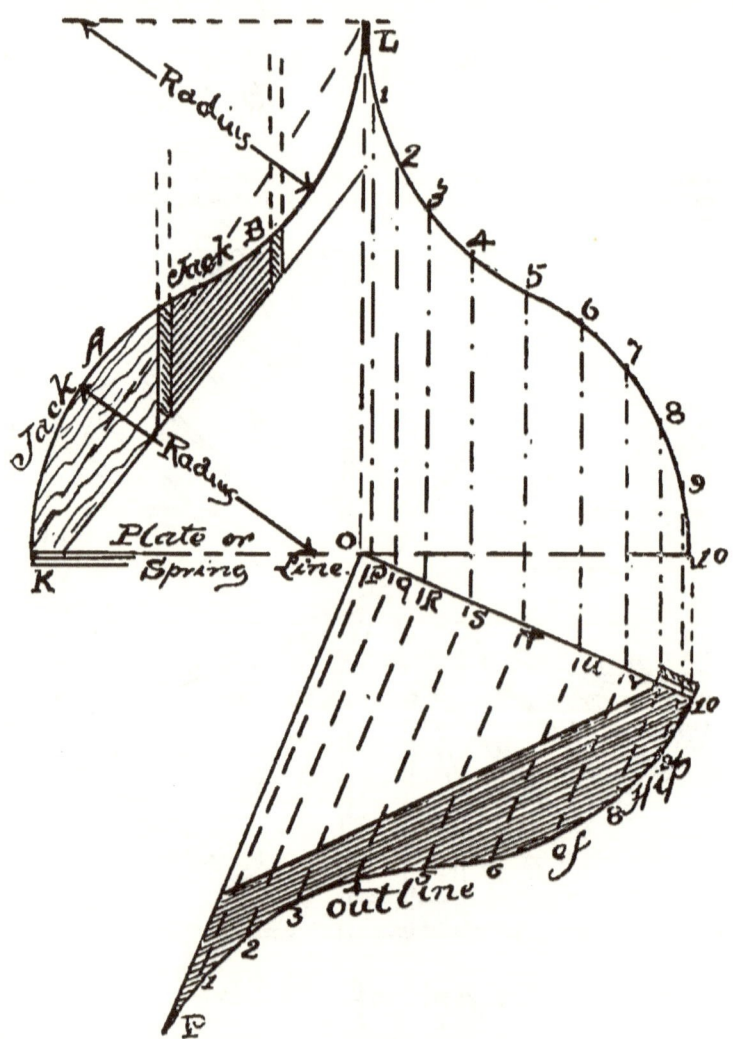

FIG. 30.—LAYOUT OF ROOF. One-half inch scale.

K, also at *h f,* etc. Join these points and the eight-sided figure will be given, as shown by the heavy black lines in the engraving.

By either of the above methods the plate line, C, D, E, F, G, H, I and J of the plan, Fig. 29, may be exactly laid out, or if the cuts or octagon mitres are to be found, the figures 7 and 17 on the steel square will give the cut. The writer prefers, however, to lay out roofs of this character *full size,* on an extemporized floor or drawing-board and to strike out the rafters also full size with a trammel rod, a bradawl and a pencil. K, A, B, L, Fig. 30, is the profile of the roof, K A and K B being jack rafters, which will stand over those marked on the *plan* above; A corresponding to A above, and B to B above. The bevel at X, is the side bevel of the jacks fitting against the hips, right and left. The lay-out will explain this very clearly.

To find the exact shape of the hip curve, as P 10', draw O 10', the seat of one octagon angle or hip rafter, and from O draw O P square from O to 10'. See Fig. 30. Divide the "ogee" line L 10 above into 10 equal parts with the compasses in the manner shown, commencing at L. Draw lines from the dividing points, plumb to the plate or spring line K, O 10, and produce these lines till they cut the hip seat O 10', as P, Q. R, S, T, U, V, W, then from the points where they cut draw lines down, P 1, Q 2, etc. Finally, make the heights of these lines equal to the heights on the regular "ogee" roof above, and trace the curve marked " Outline of Hip" for a pattern rafter, for all the eight hip rafters required.

As I have laid this roof out to a scale of a half an inch to the foot, students should have no difficulty in reproducing it as shown.

Readers will find in the sketch, Fig. 31, a very simple method of finding the side cuts of the jack rafters. To square across from the side of the rafter where the thickness of the jacks rest against it as shown here, and to join the opposite corners for the bevel as 1-2 and 3-4. Another way to find this cut is to develop the roof in the way I have described in previous chapters. And still another is to apply the steel square on the bottom edge, using the ordinary

octagon jack rafter cut. The plumb cut being always the same. As the jacks and common rafters have the same profile they must coincide.

CHAPTER XIII.

FRAMING AN OCTAGONAL ROOF WITH A CIRCULAR DOME.

AT Fig. 32, let A B C D E F G H, be the plan of the wall plates of the main octagonal roof and H O. G O. G N, E N, F M, E M, E L, D L, D K, C K, C V, B V, B J, A J, A I and H I, the seats of the octagonal hip raft-

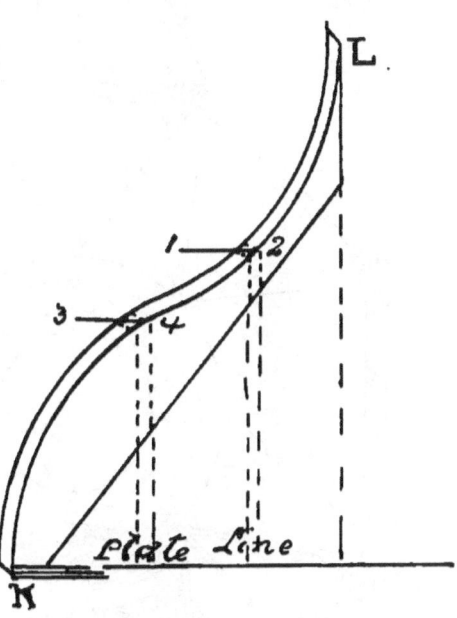

FIG. 31.

ers. The intervening planes between the hips will be circular surfaces as O N, and the rafters, if cut in horizontally as shown in the engraving, will be curved on the outer edge and each sawn to a different radius using the centre of the octagonal plan and upper circular plate J N K L M N U O I. as a fixed centre and increasing the radius for each sweep as they go down on the pitch in the manner seen in Fig. 33, where the sweeps are represented cut in between two hip rafters, the bottom cuts of which rest at the angle of hip; this will also be seen on the plan Fig. 32, as G O and G N. The upper ends or cuts of the octagonal hips are cut to, and notched under, the upper circular plate which carries the studding, forming the drum of the dome.

Concerning the length of the hips, jacks. and common rafters, readers will find the simplest method of determining their length to be that shown on the diagram Fig. 32. To obtain the length of the main hips as G N, and so on, lay off the seat F M, and square up from M. as M R. Join R F, which will be the exact length of the hip, to scale. and R, and E, will be the top and bottom bevels. For the common rafter as 3 N, divide F E into two equal parts at P, square up from P as P M, and from M square up as

M Q, and join P Q, which will be the length of the common rafter to stand over the seat 3 N. For the jacks from P, on the line P M, set off the distances from the line of the outside of the plate as 1, 2, or 4 and 5 to the point where each comes against the side of the seat of the hips G N, and F N, as P Y, P. W.

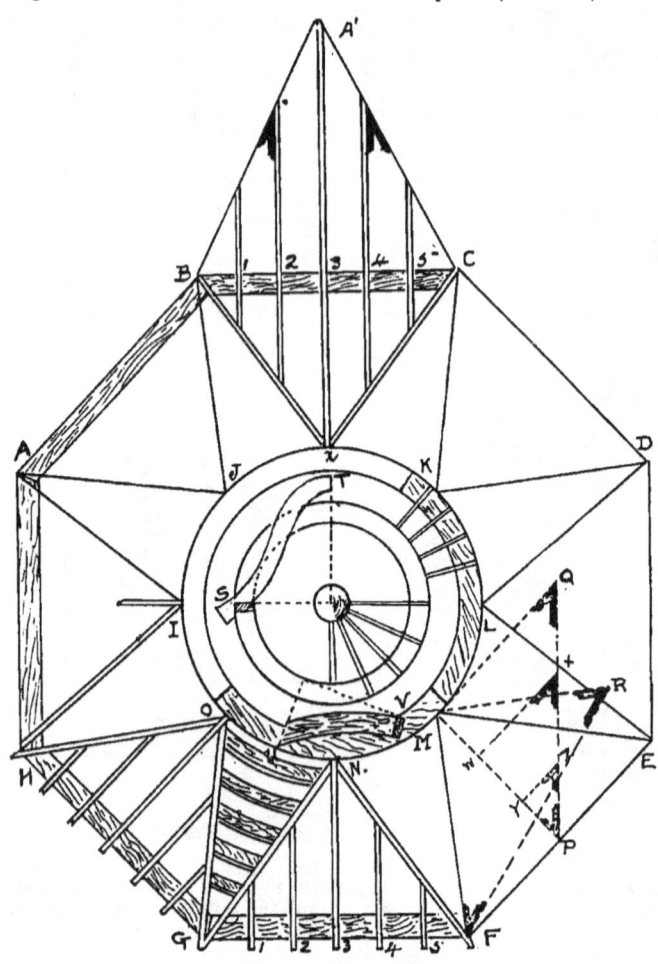

Fig. 32.

From the points W, and Y, square out till each line cuts the line P Q, at X and Z; P X and P Z, will be the exact length of each jack to the longest point.

The curved stud for the drum U V, in Fig. 32, shows how the design of the roof may be made more graceful by introducing curved studs instead of the straight studs seen in Fig. 33.   S T shows the O G rafters of the top or *dome*, and with its rise and rim. A' B C on the top side of the engraving illustrates how this roof may be developed in the way I have illustrated and explained in the previous chapters, as I have by slow degrees led up from the simplest to intricate roofs and their framing.

CHAPTER XIV.

To Frame a High Pitched or Church Roof.

AT Fig. 34 let A, B, C, D, E, F, G, H, I, J, K and L be the plan of the wall plates Around to B will be a circular end. B Y the pitch or length of common rafter which will space along the plate from B to C and from A to L. The bevel at Y will be the length which will be found to be the same length as B Y.

C P, F P, L P and I P are the seats of the valley rafters with the jacks which will fit against all four. I have drawn these on one side only as the other three are duplicate rafters with the cuts reversed. The top cut is the same as Y, and the bottom side cut as W, which may be found by developing the roof. Z is the top cut of the valley found by raising up the pitch P Z equal to X Y and joining Z I and Z C, and bevel at C the bottom cut of valleys.

In order to develop the planes of the roof produce the line C T B to any length. Produce A X B to N and with a pair of compasses strike the arc N Y cutting B N at N, through N draw N U R parallel to C T B and produce S T to

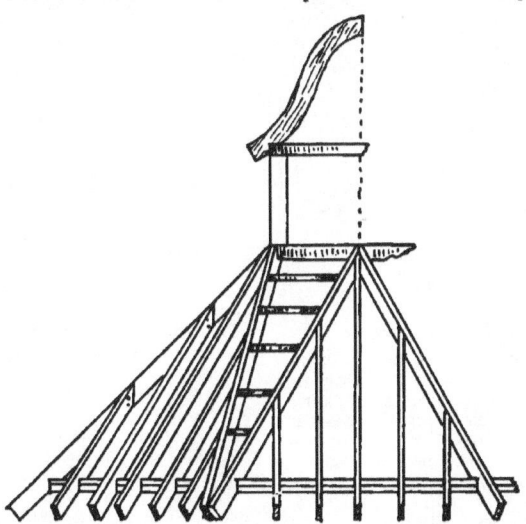

FIG. 33.

one required for the top cut against the ridge and that at B the bevel for and on the wall plate. Similar rafters will require to be cut for the semi-circular end and they will be spaced out equally round it as I have drawn them half way round from B to 8. On account of the fitting the top or peak ends of these rafters where they group at the top it is advisable to insert a circular boss or block to fit them against; the half thickness of this block must be cut from the ends of the rafters on the plumb cut. This is shown at X in the engraving. The ridge X Y will also require to be fitted to it and the common side rafters A X and B X. S T is the common rafter square to the plate and T U its exact

U, also draw P through Q to R, and set off the valley and jacks in the manner shown. Next set a pair of dividers to one of the spaces round B 8 and set off the eight equal spaces from B to O. Join N O. If the whole diagram be laid out on a sheet of Bristol or cardboard a model may be made and the system proven by cutting entirely the cardboard with a penknife or chisel from A to B, thence to O, then to N, N to R. R to P, P to C and so on as before described. The shape of the covering boards as may be determined by taking Y, as centre and with length Y A striking the sweep Y M, then setting off on Y M, 16 spaces each equal in length to 1, 2, etc.

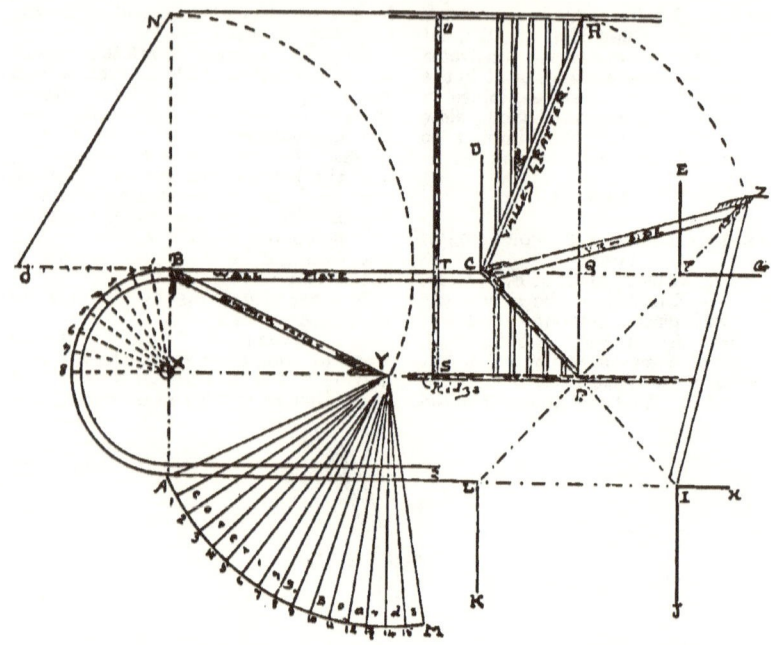

FIG. 34—LAYOUT OF A HIGH PITCHED ROOF.

CHAPTER XV.

TO FRAME A MANSARD ROOF.

BEFORE commencing to describe the proper methods to follow in framing and raising a *Mansard* roof, I will first explain what a Mansard roof is. This form of roof derived its name from being constantly used by one Francis Mansard, an architect who died in France in the year 1666. He was not, as is generally supposed, its inventor, as the idea had been previously adopted by such men as Segallo and Michael Angelo, in Italy.

The principal reason for the use of the Mansard form is to lessen the excessive height of a roof without resorting to a truss, and to obtain room space in the roof itself.

To describe or lay out a true Mansard roof, at Fig. 35, let C F, be the true height of the roof equal to half the width on the plate line C B. Draw D E, parallel to A B, and make D F, and F E, equal to A C, and C B. Join A D, and E B. Divide D F, and F E, into three equal parts and join A B, and B D. Make F G, equal to d E, and join b G,

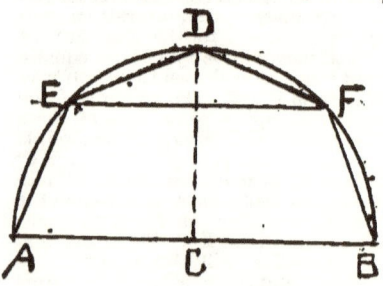

FIG. 35—LAYOUT OF A TRUE MANSARD ROOF.

FIG. 36—LAYOUT OF A MANSARD OR CURB ROOF.

and G D, thus obtaining the true form of the Mansard roof.

At Fig. 36 another way to describe this roof is shown, and this resembles more the old colonial, or what is called the American curb roof. To describe

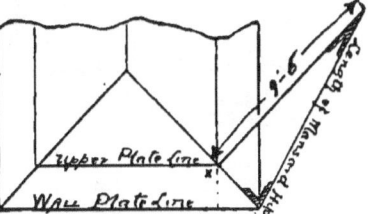

it strike the semi-circle A E D F B, from the centre C, with C D, as radius. Divide the semi-circle into 4 equal parts at E D, and F, and join A E, E D, D F, and F B, which will give the proportional form of the roof.

Fig. 38 will give readers a full conception of the framing timbers of a Mansard roof as they will appear when raised. They consist of the usual wall plate and an upper plate which is supported by the *flaring* or sloping side rafters which

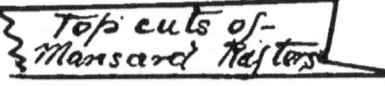

FIG. 40—TO FIND LENGTH OF MANSARD HIP.

form the Mansard chamber or attic within. Reference to the cross-section, Fig. 37, will make it clearer to the mechanic, as A. is the wall plate, E, the upper or Mansard plate supported by the Mansard or flaring rafters C, which flares 2 feet off the perpendicular. D, is

FIG. 41.

the *deck* or upper rafters, and B, a tie or ceiling beam which gives a good attic room. Half the roof only, namely, the left side, is shown in this cross-section, Fig. 37.

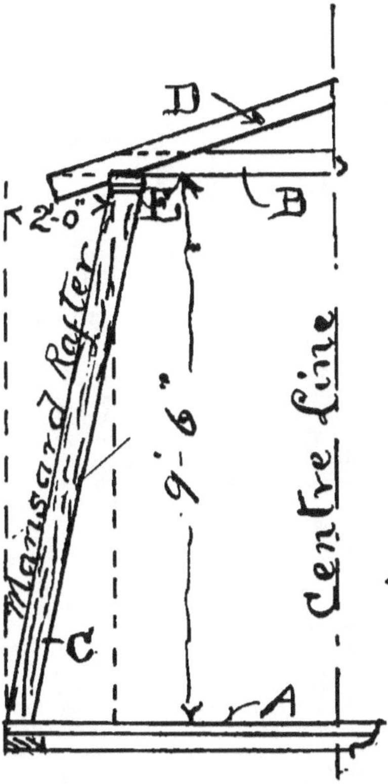

FIG. 37—CROSS SECTION OF ROOF.

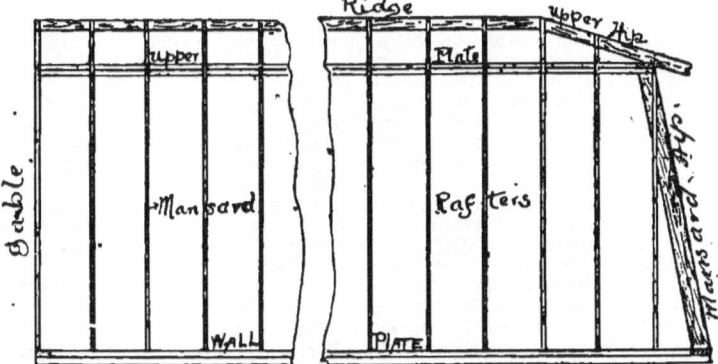

FIG. 38—ELEVATION OF FRAMING.

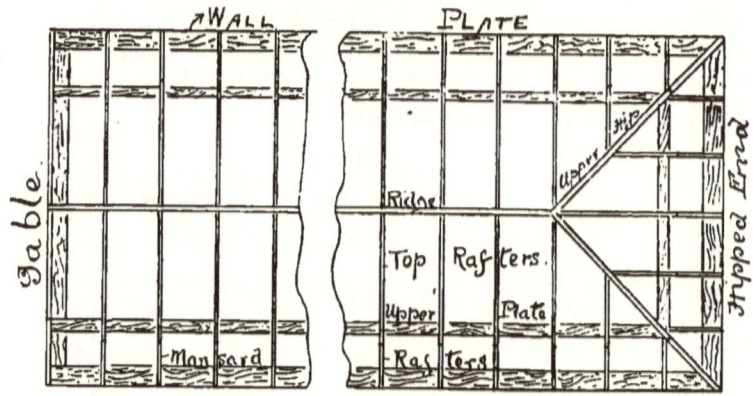

FIG. 39—PLAN OF MANSARD RAFTERS.

A comparison between the plan Fig. 39. and the elevation and cross-section will make clear the full construction of the roof and enable any mechanic to lay out, frame and raise roofs of this class. The elevation and plan show one end (the right) hipped and the other (the left) gabled. In order to determine the exact length of the Mansard hip rafter, the method is illustrated in Fig 40. It is simply to raise up on the seat X Z. of the hip the height of the pitch 9 feet and 6 inches, and to join this height with Z.

The deck or upper rafters are framed in the way I previously described. Fig. 41 represents the proper shape to frame the top cuts of Mansard rafters to prevent their slipping under the upper plate.

CHAPTER XVI.

HEMISPHERICAL DOMES.

THE roof presented to readers of this chapter is one well worthy of careful study and working out. It is of a kind which occurs on many houses now-a-days on the tops of towers for domes, etc. I should therefore recommend that those who have leisure time work it out on a board to a large scale.

A, B, C, D, E, F, G, Fig. 42, is the plan, a perfect circle, of twelve feet diameter or six feet radius, A D and B F two diameters or centre lines intersecting in the centre. The dome is hemispherical or half a ball, or sphere, therefore the elevation H J I. is struck from a six foot radius. A pair of trammel points and rod may be used in striking out these curves, but, should these

be lacking, a ¼ by ¾ inch strip and a couple of brad awls will do the job very handily.

H, I, are the plates made of thicknesses of stuff, and I J one pattern rafter. J is the top cut and I the bottom cut. They are, of course, similar. The rafters for this roof may be gotten out of 1½ or 2 inch stuff, fastened at the joint by a cleat as shown at I J. There will be eight rafters required (if it is intended to cover it vertically) as B X, C X, D X, E X. F X, G X, H X. 3 X, and these will have horizontal sweeps nailed in between them denoted here by 1. 2, 3, 4, 5, in the elevation. The exact position of these sweeps is determined by dividing the quarter circle H J into six equal parts and then from the division points. drawing lines parallel to H I. These will be the centre lines of the edges of the sweeps.

Similarly they are shown on the plan below as 1, 2. 3, 4, 5. to X F. which is as they will look from above. Their exact length for each course from 1 to 5 will be found by measuring the sweeps from A X to G X. deducting half the thickness of the rafters on each end. Patterns should be made for each course as it will be seen that each is struck from a different radius, shortening as they ascend to the top. 1 in the plan corresponding to 1 in the elevation and so on up. It will. therefore, be clearly understood how to frame such a roof as this when boarded or covered vertically.

To find the exact shape and size of the covering boards, take any one of the six divisions and set it off on each side of G, the point where X G, cuts the quarter circle A F, at G; produce X G, indefinitely. Now, with the dividers set off on G S, the six distances, H I, 1 2, 2 3, 3 4, 4 5, 5 J; and draw lines from these points square to G S. Next again with the dividers make these squared lines each equal in length those dotted lines passing through G X, from T to U, and draw the curves as shown, which will give the exact length and curvature of the boards to be bent round I J. There will be 12 of these for each quarter circle on plan or 24 for the whole roof. If this be laid out on a cardboard sheet it will be found to fit exactly.

To cover this roof horizontally, all the rafters, 24 in number, must be set vertically or plumb, as B X, 1 X, 2 X, etc., to A X, and it would be best to have a finial or block at the top to receive the top ends of the rafters. In order to find the shape of the level covering boards,

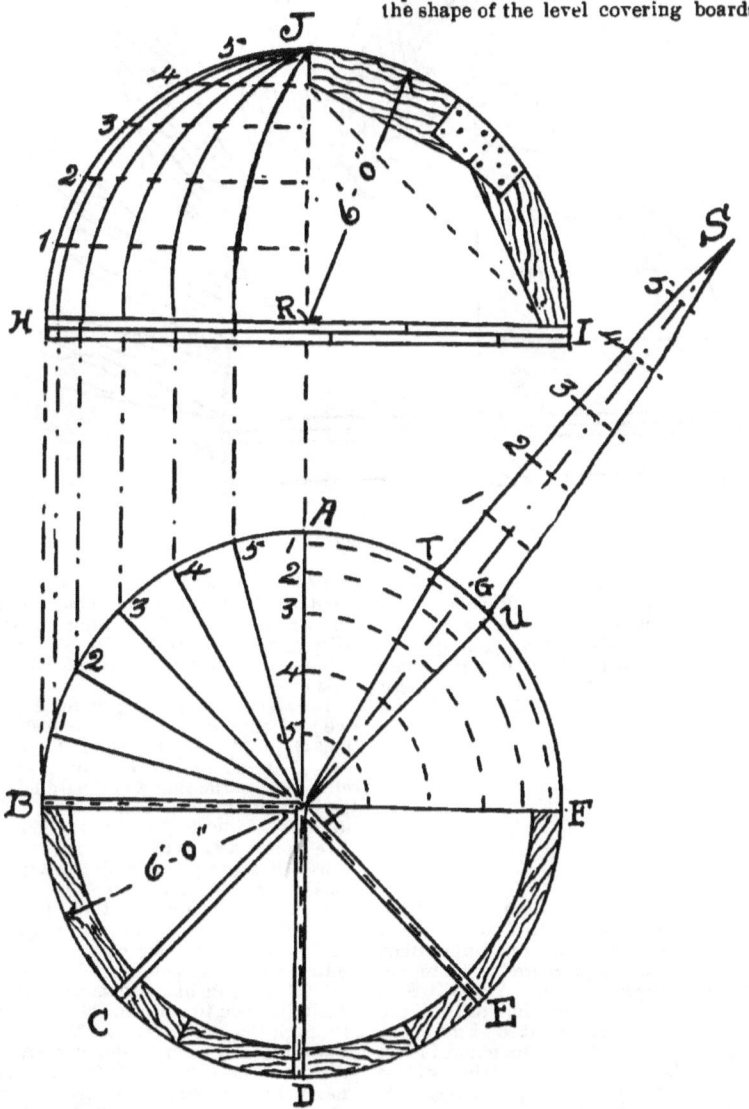

FIG. 42.

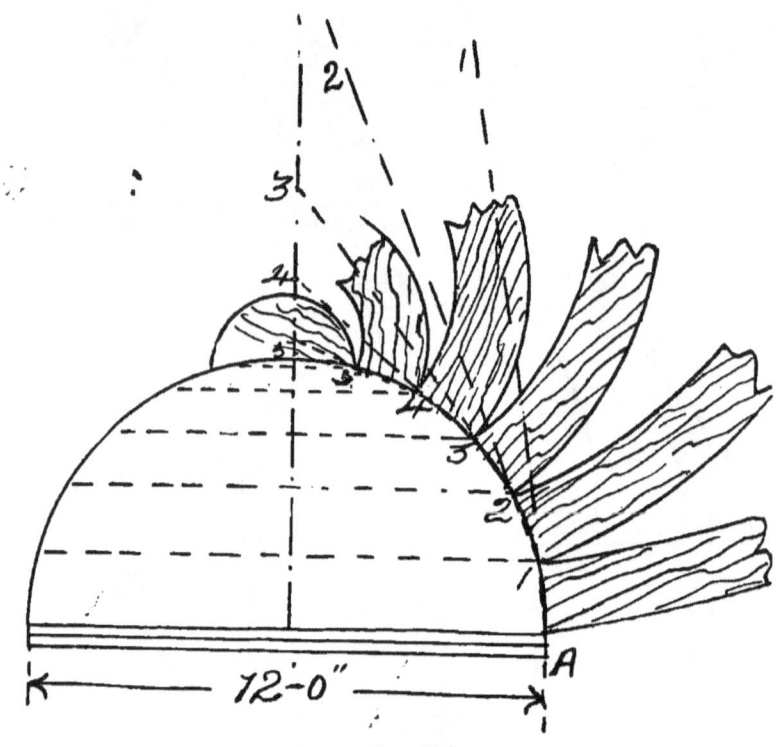

Fig. 43.

divide the curve Fig. 43, into 6 equal
parts and draw line from division points
parallel to plate. Join A 1, 1 2, 2 3, 3 4,
4 5, 5 6, and produce these joining lines
till they cut the centre line produced
indefinitely. The points where these
produced lines intersect the centre line
will be the centres for the curves of the
covering boards as represented in the
engraving.

CHAPTER XVII.

To Frame a Circular Elliptic Dome.

READERS will observe that I have
here treated a roof with which
most mechanics are unfamiliar,
and it is a pleasure for me to describe it for this reason. A C D B, Fig.
44, is the plan or outside line of the
plates which measure 12' 0" x 20' 0", or
the roof will be 20 feet long and 12 feet
wide. Across I K R its section will be
a semi-circle, or A E B and across F K
S its section will be a semi-*ellipse* (not
an *oval*, as this figure is often mis-

called). As there may probably be some
readers who are not acquainted with the
proper methods of striking a semi-
ellipse, as H M L H C really is we will
proceed to illustrate and describe the
best in use.

In referring to the engraving, Fig. 45,
we will suppose A B to be 20 feet long
and C D 6 feet equal to the E F on Fig.
44. Now to find exact curve of the
ellipse draw the line E C F parallel to A
D B, and draw F E and B F. Now
divide the sides E C and C F each into
five equal parts as 1 2 3 4 and E and join
these dividing points with the angle A,
as 4A, 3A, 2A, 1A. and CA. Similar
lines are drawn on the other side to B.
After this is done, divide the sides A E
and BF each into five equal parts and
join the dividing points with C, as AC,
1C, 2C, etc ; do likewise on the side BF.
Next proceed to trace the elliptic curve
through the points where the joining
lines intersect each other, as shown in
the diagram, Fig. 45. This is the exact
method of drawing an ellipse, but as it
is not always applicable in the case of
large spans like on this roof I would

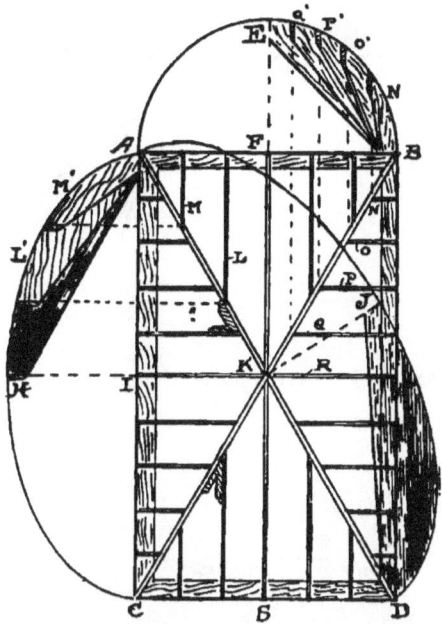

line on the under side. Fig. 47 gives another, but less accurate, method of obtaining this curve. AB is the length, CD the height. Take a rod and set off the length AC from D on the line AB. This will give the two face or points E and F. Drive nails or pins into these points and to them attach a string which will reach exactly to D. Now place a pencil inside the string at D and trace the curve as shown. This is a very simple way to gain an elliptic curve, but is not a very true one on account of the stretching of the string. It is, however, good enough for small curves. Where the trammel is not available *ellipses cannot possibly be accurately described* with compasses.

Having described the best methods of striking out elliptic curves we will refer back to Fig. 44. We find the cross and longitudinal or length sections to be a circle and an ellipse. Now to frame the dome join BC and AD on the plane, and on each side of the centre line set off half the thickness of the hips—inch, inch and a-half or two inches, according to the thickness. Next draw the seats of the jack rafters, nine on each side, and five on each end, reaching from the plates to the hips.

To find the necessary outline of the hip rafters, which, being the intersection of an ellipse and a semi-circle will be also of elliptic form, from the centre K, raise up the height K J, equal to H I, and proceed to strike the curve by any of the methods described; A J D, J D, will be the outline of the top edge of the hip rafter. For the jacks draw lines from the hips on the seat lines cutting the quadrant E B, in N, O P Q, which will give the exact lengths of the semi-circular jacks N, on plan; O, on section, to O, on plan, and so on up to R, which

recommend mechanics to use the trammel method illustrated in Fig. 46. The trammel is made of two pieces of grooved stuff halved together in the way denoted by the heavy black lines in the engraving. In the groove two little runners slide, and to them is loosely attached a rod as ACB in Fig. 46. The distance from A to B, Fig. 46, is equal to half the long diameter of the ellipse, or from A to I or I to C, on Fig. 44, and the distance from C to B is the same as the height on from I to H, on Fig 44. At B the pencil is placed, and being moved round, as it were, the slides run in the grooves and the pencil follows and outlines the desired elliptic curve. By means of the trammel the full ellipse may be outlined as shown by the dotted

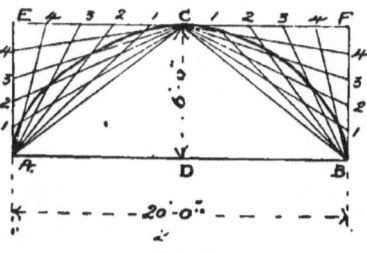

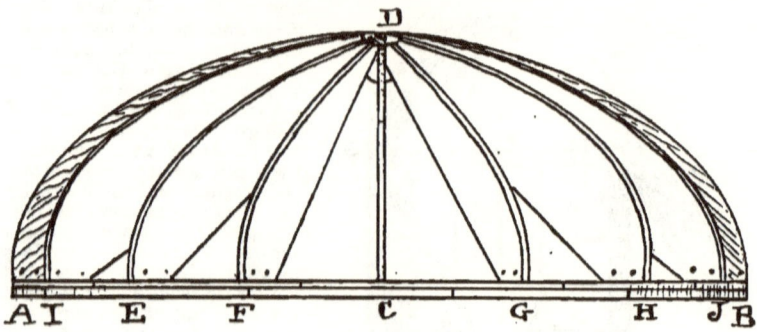

ELLIPTICAL RAFTERS, RAISED.

FIG. 50.

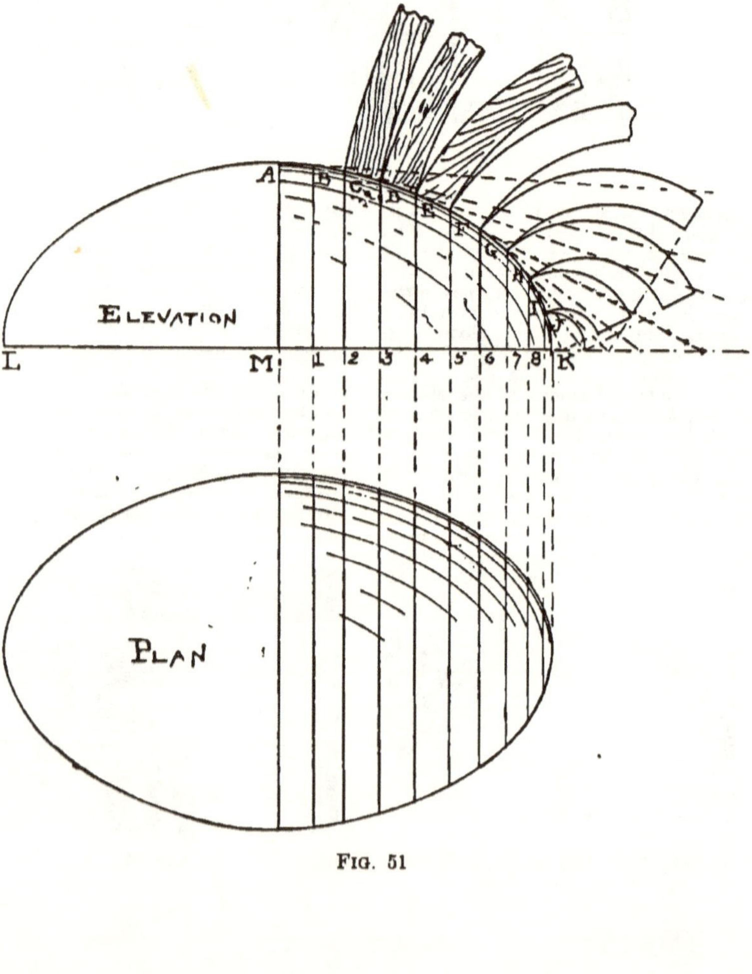

ELEVATION

PLAN

FIG. 51

rafter will be a quadrant as E B. In the same way the two elliptic jack rafters on each side of K F, as M, and L, are found by the dotted lines. The plumb cuts will be, as usual, plumb, and the side bevels will be those seen on the plan. To those who have the time and patience, I would recommend that they make scale models of these roofs from

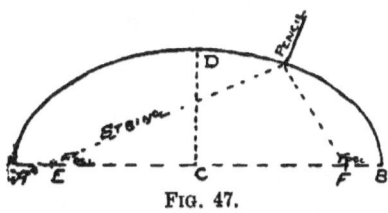

FIG. 47.

the descriptions given in previous chapters and in this. Nothing verifies and proves the value of a system of lines like an accurate model or true representation of the actually constructed roof on a small scale, and it is my great desire to publish nothing which is not both accurate and necessary.

CHAPTER XVIII.

To Frame an Elliptic Dome With an Elliptic Plan.

AT Fig. 49, the plan of the elliptic roof, let A B C D E F G H I J K L M N O and P be its shape on the outside line of the elliptic plate, cut in sweeps as shown in the engraving. In striking this plan, any of the methods which I described in the last chapter, or by the simple and accurate method which I here illustrate at Fig. 48. It consists of one horizontal straight edge A B, tacked on the floor on the line of the major axis or long diameter of the ellipse, and a second straight edge C E,

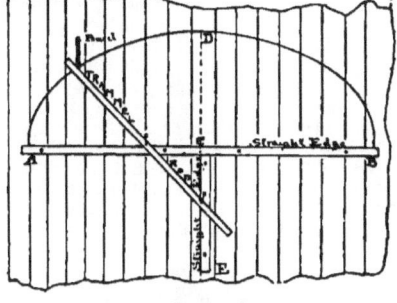

FIG. 48.

set on the minor axis or short diameter below it. These are represented in the engraving. A trammel rod or tracer is made with the distance from the pencil to the farthest nail against the short straight equal to A C or half the long diameter, and the distance from the pencil to the nearest nail sliding against the long straight edge, equal to C D or half the short diameter. The elliptic curves may by this method be accurately struck to the size desired.

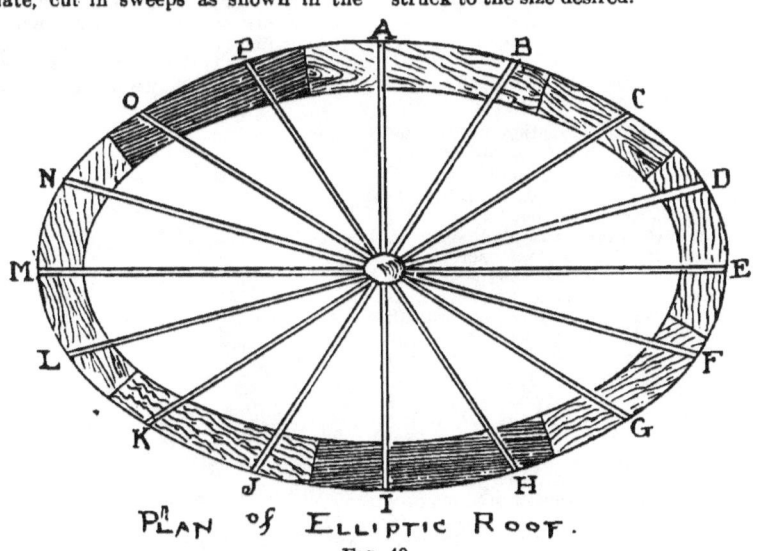

PLAN of ELLIPTIC ROOF.

FIG. 49.

In this dome roof I have inserted a boss in the centre to receive the top cuts of the elliptic rafters, all of which radiate from the centre to the outside edge of the plate terminating at A B C D, etc. The rafters which will stand over the plan, Fig. 49, on M E will be A D and D B on Fig. 50, which is the projection or view of elliptic rafters nailed in position.

Each set of two rafters, as AI, BJ, CK, DL, Fig. 49, etc., must be struck out separately with the major axis or long diameter of each, being the plan length as AI, BJ, etc., with the minor as CD, Fig. 50; great care and accuracy is necessary in striking out each set so as to have them, the curves, absolutely correct and appear as at Fig. 50 when raised.

In order to determine the shape of the covering boards or roof covering proceed to Fig. 51 and draw the long diameter LMK, also the short diameter MA, and

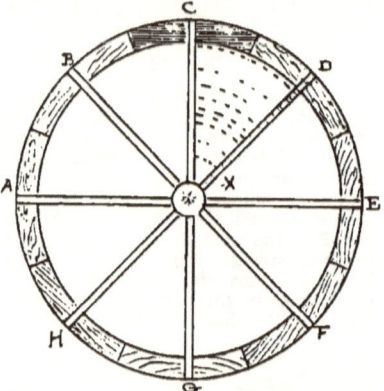

FIG. 52.—PLAN OF PLATE, RAFTERS AND SWEEP.

strike the elliptic elevation of the roof LAK. Divide the quarter ellipse into ten equal divisions as denoted by A B C D E F G H I J K and let fall lines square to M K as A M, B1, C2, etc., and produce these across the plan below, to represent 10 boards bent across the rafters. To find the exact shape of these covering boards join the division points on the curve A K, and produce each till it cuts the line M K produced. The points where these lines intersect will be the centres from which the curved boards, which are necessary to bend across the rafters, may be struck in the way represented in the engraving, Fig. 51. For the purpose of fully proving the correctness of the above methods I would urge upon mechanics to make a scale model as before in cardboard of this roof, thus proving the exactness of the methods set forth in the foregoing.

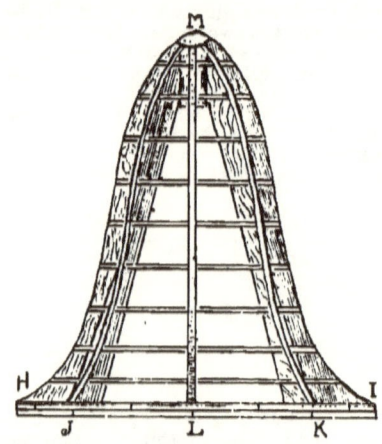

FIG. 53.—MOLDED RAFTERS, PLATE AND SWEEPS.

CHAPTER XIX.

FRAMING A CIRCULAR MOLDED ROOF TOWER.

HAVING before described the proper methods to be followed in framing a straight sided or conical roof with a circular base of plan, in this chapter I will give readers the information necessary to know in laying out and framing a roof with a molded form of rafter. As there are many of these constructed now-a-days it will no doubt be welcome to studious mechanics.

By referring to Fig. 52 it will be seen that the plate or plan is a complete circle, as A B C D E F G H, made up in two thicknesses of sweeps cut out as I

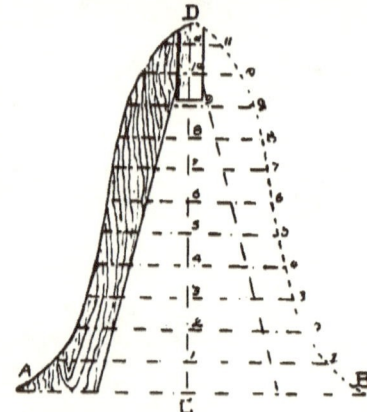

FIG. 54.—HOW TO LAY OUT CURVE OF RAFTERS.

have shown by the joint lines. The molded rafters (of a bell shape) are, as seen on plan, eight in number and must be made exactly to the curvature repre-

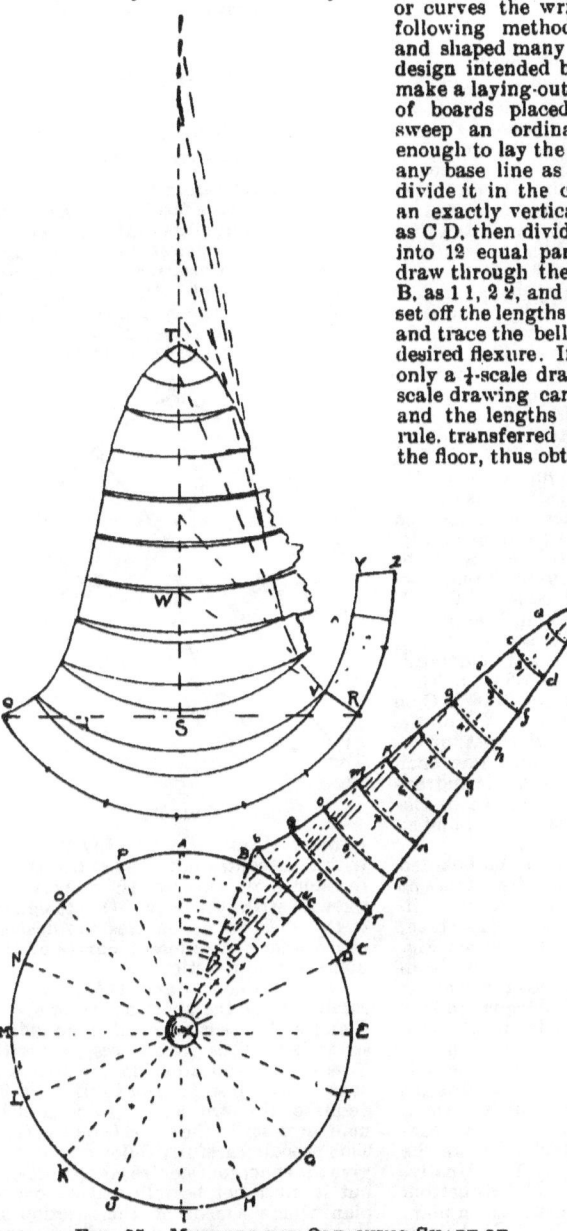

sented on the projected framing of the roof or rafters, etc., raised as seen at Fig 53.

In order to obtain the exact flexure or curves the writer has followed the following method with much success and shaped many molded rafters to the design intended by the architect; 1st, make a laying-out floor out of a number of boards placed level on planks, or sweep an ordinary floor clean, big enough to lay the roof out in, and draw any base line as A B in Fig. 54; also divide it in the centre at C, and draw an exactly vertical or plumb line to it, as C D. then divide the height line C D into 12 equal parts as 1 2 3, etc., and draw through these lines parallel to A B, as 1 1, 2 2, and so on up to 11. Now set off the lengths 1 1, 2 2, and so on up, and trace the bell-shaped curves to the desired flexure. If the architect furnish only a ¼-scale drawing of the roof, the scale drawing can be similarly lined off and the lengths taken with the scale rule. transferred and relaid on out on the floor, thus obtaining the curve.

When the curve is laid out on a drawing-board the pattern rafter is made by placing the planks on the lines and marking on it the length before as described and in the manner illustrated in Fig. 54, where a rafter sawn out is delineated on the left hand side, as A D, and the thickness of the 6-inch boss at D, which is inserted for the purpose of giving a better nailing at the peak, is taken from the top cut. This boss is also seen on the plan, Fig. 52 at X, and on the projection of set-up rafters, Fig. 53 at M, where it is obviously necessary in order to obtain a firm nailing for the top ends of the molded rafters. At Fig. 53 the mechanic will see how a series of circular strips or sweeps as they are

FIG. 55.—METHODS FOR OBTAINING SHAPE OF COVERING BOARDS.

technically termed, are nailed in, ranging from the plate to the peak. These are essential when it is intended to board the roof from bottom to top, for the purpose of nailing the boards to them.

They are sweeps or arcs of circles and struck from different radii, decreasing as they go up. This will be readily understood by studying the plan, Fig. 52, where the dotted lines represent the outside edges of the sweeps shown on Fig. 53. As there are 8 intervening spaces between the rafters. and there are 9 in the height, there will be 72 needed altogether or 8 of each kind, and they may be solidly nailed in the way indicated in the engraving, Fig. 53.

This form of roof may be covered in two ways, either vertically or horizontally. When covered vertically, the sweeps described above are inserted and the shape of the covering boards determined, in the following manner. Let A B C D E F G H I J K L M N O P on Fig. 55 be the plan of the outside edge of the circular plate. and A X, C X, E X, G X, I X, K X, M X, and O X be the rafters, all abutting against the boss X, on plan, in the manner seen at D, Fig. 54; also suppose the dotted lines on Fig. 54 represent the outside edges of the sweeps. Now to determine the shape of one covering board, produce X C to U and on the line E U. taking U as centre, proceed to strike the arcs *a b, c d. e f, g h, i j. k l, m n, o p, q r, s t* cutting U C at the points 1 2 3 4 5 6 7 8 9 10. Then set off on each side of the line U C on each arc the distances from X B on the plan, *taking the exact full length of the curve* and *not* on a straight line, each corresponding as shown in the engraving. For instance, *s c t* must be the full length of the curve B C D, and so on with each all the way up.

If the roof is intended to be boarded horizontally then more rafters must be inserted, in order to give a better nailing. and this roof will then need sixteen, instead of only eight, as before, see Fig. 55. To obtain the shape of the horizontal covering boards, proceed to the upper engraving and draw Q R equal to M E below, and S T vertical to it. Also set off the bell-shaped curves as shown.

To find the shape of the first or bottom board, assume R V to be a straight line, and produce it till it cuts the vertical line S T at W, then with W as centre and radii W R and W V, strike the two arcs Q R Z and Q V Y. Finally, to find the exact length of this bottom board, take any curved distance on plan, as A B. Fig. 55, and set it off eight times from Q to Z, as indicated by the marks.

This will give half way round, which doubled will give entire circular covering board for the first section. By continuing this process up to the top, all the horizontal boards may be laid out.

CHAPTER XX.

To Frame a Gothic Tower Roof of Four-Centre Section.

I HERE set before readers. a form of roof which is fast becoming popular on account of its uniform curves.

As the section of the roof is a combination of curves, we must first proceed to lay it out. On a large floor or platform draw the *spring line* AB, Fig. 56. Divide this line AB into 4 equal parts as 1, 2. 3 and 4; also from A and

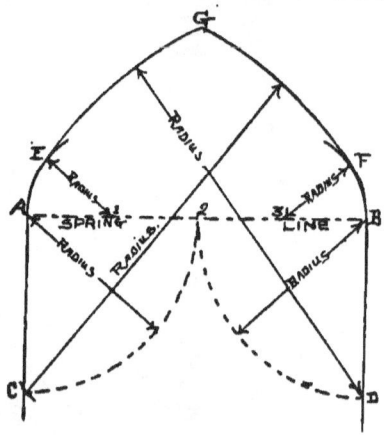

FIG. 56.

B, draw AC and BD square to AB. Now with A as centre and A2 as radius strike the curve 2C, cutting AC at point C, likewise strike the curve 2D cutting BD at D. This process locates the desired centres for the different curves of the dome or tower section.

With 1 as centre and 1 A length of radius, strike the short curve, or arc A E and with 3 as centre and same radius strike B F. This gives 2 arcs, next with C as centre, and allowing the *trammel pencil* to be just *tangent* to B F at F, describe the arc F G. In a similar manner describe the arc E G on the left. This process carefully followed out will give the exact four-centre gothic section, but it must not be followed in every plan where a roof of this section is shown, as the position of the centres may not be placed or divided off as is shown above, and a detail or layout of the roof may be necessary to determine their position. The foregoing description, however, will make the work familiar and easy.

In order to lay out the rafters for this roof, proceed to Fig. 57, and lay out the plan full size A B C D, also draw the diagonals A D and B C, the seats of the hips, with the jacks *a b c d e f g h i j*, against the hip seat *c* X. On the line B D, divided in half at E. raise up the gothic section line, and from this section make a paper or wood pattern rafter to the curve B 12. in the manner shown in the engraving. Divide B 12, into twelve equal parts, as 1, 2, 3, 4, etc., and from each division point draw a line square to the line B E D, and produce these lines to the hip seat.

B 12, will, of course, be the common rafter standing over E X. Each jack will, because the hip rafter is on a mitre or angle of 45 degrees, be shorter as they go down from X to C, and their lengths will be as K 11. L 10, M 9, N 7, and so on down to B.

At Fig. 58, readers will see a comparatively simple method which may be followed to obtain the top side bevel of the jack rafters. A B. is the common, showing its upper edge. Set off rafter No. 10 from A to C, C D, being the ver-

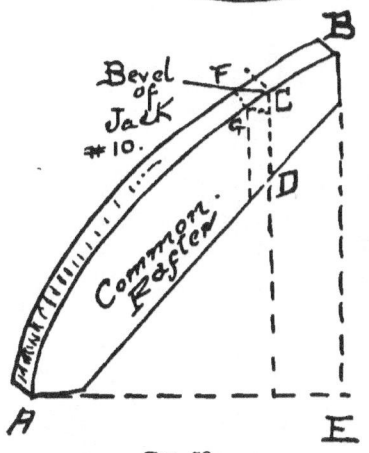

FIG. 58.

tical or plum cut. Square across from the upper edge corner, from G to C, as C F, and from C D, set off the thickness of the jack rafter, 2 inches, or 3 inches, or whatever it may be. The bevel will be as shown in the engraving.

B X. From the points where these dotted lines cut B X, draw up square to B X, lines of an indefinite length. Now, commencing from B, on line B E, take the first division 1, and set off the height from the line to 1, on the first line on the hip seat, also height at 2, 3, 4, 5, and so on up to 12. To be explicit, I would say transfer these heights from perpendiculars on B E, to perpendiculars on B X. Next trace the curve, F B, through the points 12, 11, 10, etc., and the proper outline of hip rafter will be found.

CHAPTER XXI.

To Frame a Trussed Roof of Large Span on the Balloon Principle.

THAT carpentry is a progressive art is a truism that the observer will not hesitate to admit, and a careful examination of the timber structures being erected in the United States to-day will impress the examiner with the fact that it is also a liberal art. This is, without doubt, one of the chief reasons why wood has not been entirely driven out of the field by its great competitor, iron, as it can be readily and economically employed where the latter

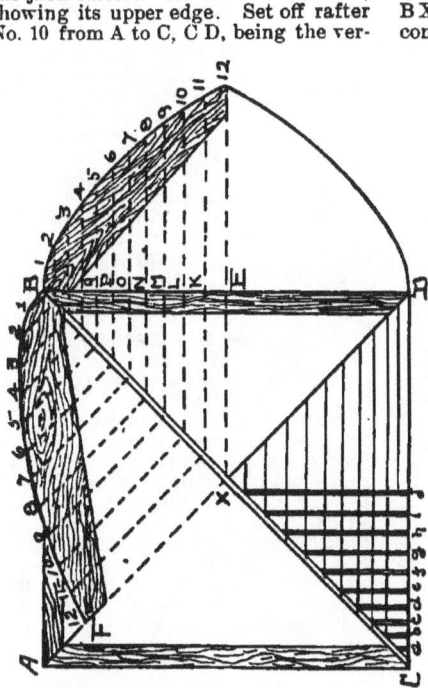

FIG. 57.

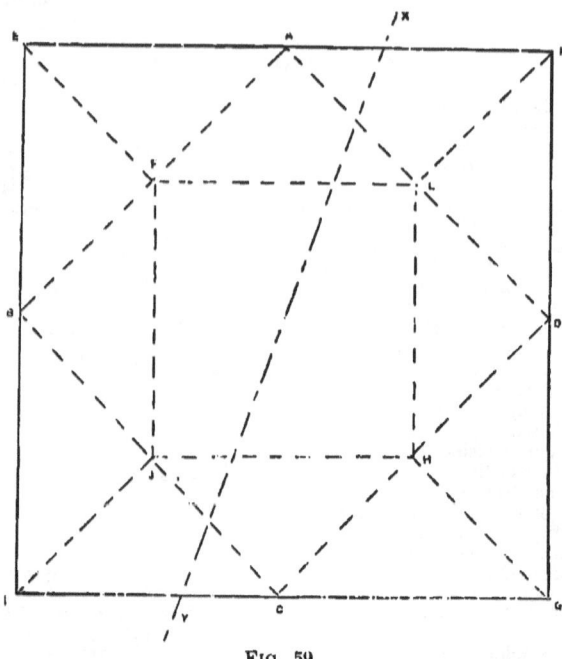

FIG. 59.

material would be inadaptable. The numerous and exceedingly artistic dwellings which are erected in all parts of the country attest this, and while designing them the architects have endeavored to devise new forms of construction which might enable them to produce an effective design and at the same time be a cheap one to build. An illustration of this will be seen in the sketches which are here introduced, as they explain a unique method of balloon framing which was adopted in a church, the building being a frame structure, and having an auditorium measuring 50 feet square. The architect wished to avoid inserting the usual form of trusses and, after careful study, he devised the manner of construction here shown. Fig. 59 is the plan of the auditorium, E A D G C I B E being the outside line. B F A, A L D, D H C and C J B are the trusses which the reader will notice do not span the roof at right angles in the way generally followed, but are placed at an angle of 45 degrees across the angle of the corner. Each of these were 25 feet on base line and were framed in the way represented in the isometrical projected view (see frontispiece), without any tie beam, yet of a form statically strong enough to support the rafters and shingling placed upon it. They were then placed diagonally across the plan so that their seats formed a square, as it were, within a square. This the reader will comprehend better by referring again to Fig. 59, where the dotted lines A D, D C, C B and B A, are the seats of the trusses, and a close observation of the projection (see frontispiece), will give him a perfect idea of how they were positioned. The hip rafters E F, K, D, G H and I J, rested against the trusses which supported on their peaks the upper wall plate or purlin on which the ventilator was raised, and against which the jack rafters from the trusses rested. A peculiar feature of the construction, which the reader will notice, is that the principal rafter of the trusses in each plane of three, as D I and D H, in the plane G H L K, was partly a hip and partly a valley rafter at the same time, because the jacks were cut from the plates below to them and from them to the purlin above; but the sides still formed separate planes and, when covered, showed a straight surface, as G H L K, Fig. 59. Taking the whole construction as a piece of statical and economical design, it savors more of engineering than architecture, but as an uncommon piece of roof framing it is a most ingenious method of solving an old problem in a new way.

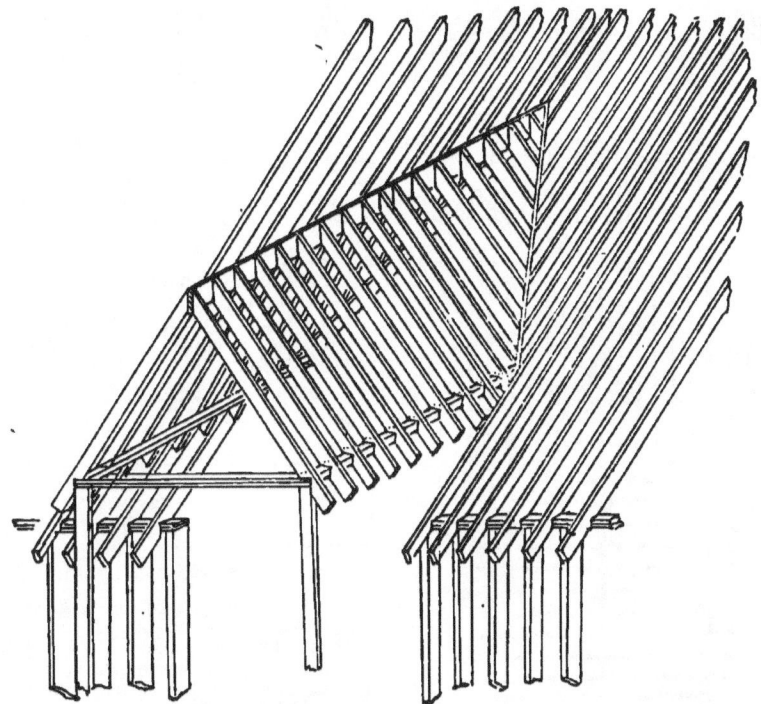

FIG. 61.—ROOF TIMBERS WHEN RAISED.

CHAPTER XXII.

TO FRAME A ROOF OF UNEQUAL HEIGHTS OF PITCHES AND PLATES.

HAVING described in previous chapters roofs springing from wall plates on the same level, I will show in this the proper method to be followed in framing two roofs where the plates are at different heights and the roofs at different pitches. These roofs to those unused to them appear very difficult to frame, but are really not so.

Fig. 61 will give readers a full conception of the timbers forming the two roofs as they will appear when "raised" or set up in their permanent position. It will be noticed that the wall-plate of the projection or bay is about four feet higher than the plate on the main wall of the house, also that the rafters are cut on different pitches.

If the reader cannot clearly understand this I would refer him to Fig. 62. which is a sectional view of the roof when raised through the line A B, on Fig. 63, the plan of roofs. Here the different levels of the plates will be seen

and another view of the rafters and stud wall of the projection. As the timbers are all marked very little description is necessary.

Concerning the methods to be followed in finding the lines for this form, it is as follows: C D E F. Fig. 63, is the plan of the extension plates, I and J being the plates of the main house wall.

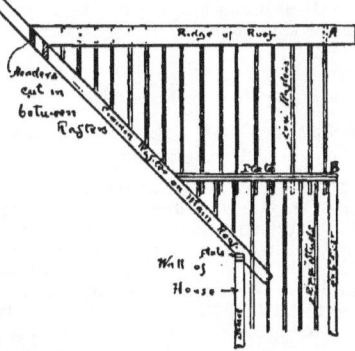

FIG. 62.—SECTION ON LINE A B.

G C and G F are the seats or plans of the valleys determined by the intersection of the two peaked roofs. To find the exact length of these valleys raise up square the pitch G K. Set off the height G K equal to A B Fig. 62, and join K F, which line is the exact length of the valley rafter as seen at Figs. 61 and 62, also the length of G C.

Next, to find the lengths of the jack rafters on each side of the valleys set a

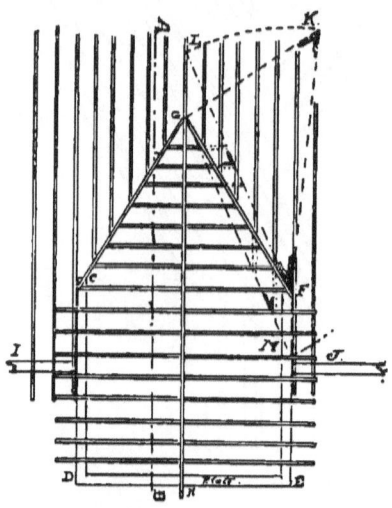

FIG. 63.—PLAN OF ROOFS.

pair of compasses to the line K F, and with F as centre cut the line H G L at L and join L F. Now if the jacks from the ridge line H G be produced to the line L F their exact length will be given with the side or top edge bevel. To obtain the length of the jack rafters on the main roof, the feet of which nail against the valleys, draw R M parallel to L F and the lengths of these jacks will be thus found.

CHAPTER XXIII.

To FRAME A HIP AND VALLEY ROOF OF UNEQUAL PITCH.

FIGURE 64 is the projection of the roofs completed, and it will be noticed that they are of different pitches and widths. A B C D E F G M H K I J, Fig. 65, is the plan of the building. A B is a gable end, and A N is the length of the common rafter; also D E is a gable end. D O being the length of the common rafter each has a ridge L N X and P O Y. The main roof

is hipped, having four principal hip rafters with jacks. The intersection of each of the L's on the building with or rather in the main roof gives three valley rafters and creates the framing problem which is to be worked out.

Proceed to lay out the plan of the plates, hips, valleys and ridges as shown on Fig. 66, and join I G and H Q giving the peak R; also draw the dotted lines K R F and M R X in Fig. 65. To obtain the length of the main hip rafters square up from R and set off on the square line the pitch height R C equal to E T. Join H S, which will be the exact length of the hip rafter, with the bevel S for the top cut and the bevel H for the bottom cut.

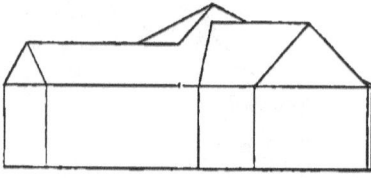

FIG. 64.—ELEVATION OF ROOF.

To find the lengths of the jacks set a pair of compasses or a rod at H and with H S as radius sweep the arc S V. Join V where the arc cuts the line R F and H, also draw the jack rafters square to the plate K H until they reach the line V H, and this line will determine their length and the bevel U will be the cut across the top of each against the hip, that at I being the plumb cut. Reverse cuts are made to go against the hip I R and G R, from the plates K I and G F.

To find the lengths of the jacks placed on the plate G M H, proceed to raise up from R square to G R, the pitch R Z; join Z G and with G as centre and radius G Z sweep the arc Z X, cutting M R N L in X; join X G. Set off the jack rafters in the manner shown, reaching from the plate G M H to the line G X and their lengths will be thus found. The bevel W will be the cut across the top edges of jacks in getting the cut to fit against the hip. It will also be the bevel reversed on the opposite to fit against the hips standing over Q R and R I.

In framing the valleys to stand over the seats X C and X J, first find out where the ridge will penetrate the main roof. This may be simply done by setting off on the line E T, the half pitch height L N and drawing out square as 1, 2. The point 2 will be the point where the ridge L N will enter the main roof. This must be transferred over to cut the ridge X; and J X, C X will be the seats of the valleys.

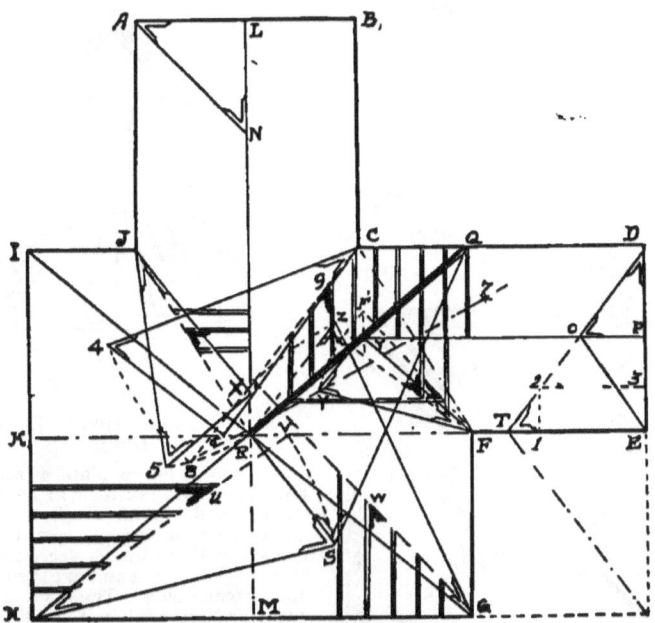

FIG. 65.—LAYOUT OF RAFTERS

To find the valley rafters, square up. from X. which will be the line X 5, on it set off the, pitch N L, and join J 5 which will be the exact length of the valley rafter with the top and bottom bevels as indicated on the diagram. It will be here seen that I have prolonged one valley from X till it cuts the centre line of the main roof and at the point where it cuts raised up the whole pitch of T E, as 6 A. This is done for the purpose of determining the lengths of the jack rafters, and is necessary to find the angle. C 6 F is the angle. To find the short jacks reaching from the hip Q R to the valley C X, join C F and divide it into two equal parts as 6 7. Now with C as centre and C 4 as radius. sweep the arc 4 8, cutting 7 6, produced at 8 and join C 8; next draw the jack rafters from R Q to the dotted line C 8, which will be their lengths and the bottom cuts across the top edge of each jack, nailing against the valley rafter 6 C, will be the bevel 9.

The jacks from the ridge L N X to the valley J X. are found similarly by setting the compasses to radius J 5 and sweeping the arc cutting the line X R; then by joining this point with J by the dotted line seen to the left of the valley, the jacks may be drawn as before.

For the valley F Y raise up square from Y the pitch Y Y equal to P O, and join Y F for the length of valley. The jacks are found by the process described before and the bevels are clearly seen. Each hip and valley rafter should be gotten out separately to avoid confusion, and the diagram closely studied as the system is simple and easily understood.

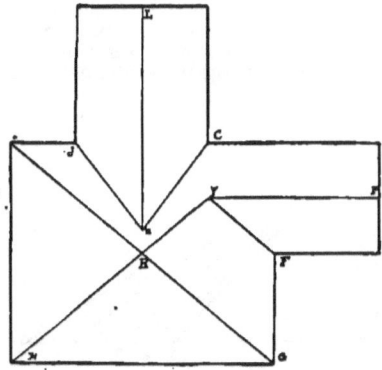

FIG. 66.—PLAN OF ROOF.

CHAPTER XXIV.

To Frame a Roof of Unequal Lengths of Rafters.

LET A B C D in Fig. 67 be the *square* plate or lower plate, which has short, or *curb* rafters supporting a *circular* plate, E F G H, on which rests a drum, or short cylindrical tower as E C D F, Fig. 69, topped by a roof with curved rafters. By referring to the plan. Fig. 67,. it will be seen that the seats of the rafters will be of differ-

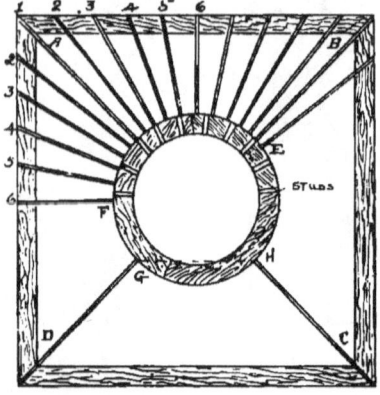

FIG. 67.—PLAN OF PLATES AND RAFTERS.

ent lengthening from the centre, or number 6, to the corner or hip rafter I. and that this occurs on all four sides of the square plate. As the seats are of different lengths the rafters will also be of different lengths. though they have the same *rise* or pitch, as X Y in Fig. 68. In this figure the different lengths of rafters will be distinctly seen decreasing in size from the hip or angle to the centre of the plate. this occurring on each side, which will necessitate 8 sets of five rafters, cut with right and left hand bevels on the plate, also one set of

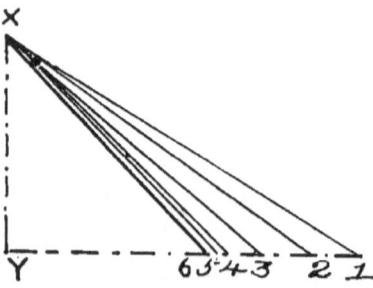

FIG. 68.—DIFFERENT LENGTHS OF RAFTERS.

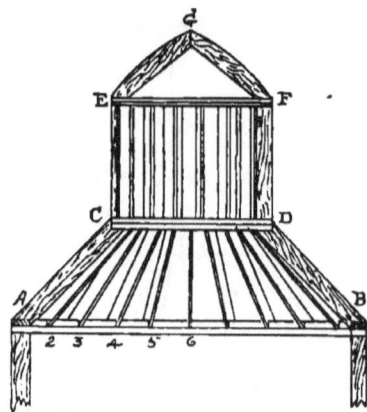

FIG. 69.—PROJECTION OF ROOF AND DRUM.

4 with square cut on plate, as number 6. Each succeeding rafter will have different top and bottom bevels, and require great care in laying out, so as to cut the timbers without waste, so that it would be wisest to lay out and cut them in sets, one for each side. The top and bottom cuts as represented in Fig. 69, are also notched to fit over the plates and thus prevent their slipping; this will also demand care in laying out, because each notch will have a different bevel. The gothic roof on the drum may be struck out to the curve shown and rafters cut out. As all the rafters are the same length, they can be sawn from one pattern, and set up in the manner which I have already described.

CHAPTER XXV.

To Frame a Roof with Pitched Ridges.

THE following roof of an unusual kind will be found of value to those carpenters who live in the country or whose duty it is to construct barns, or other special buildings, where great room is required in the roof or attic.

The engraving. Fig. 70, is an isometric view of the roof, and as will be seen it consists of a roof of four gables on a square plan, with four valleys and four ridges which rise on a pitch from the peaks of the gables and terminate at the peaks of the valleys, giving the effect as shown. The rafters of the gables are half or mitre pitch, and twelve and twelve on the steel square. The peak of the valleys represented in Fig. 71 is 4

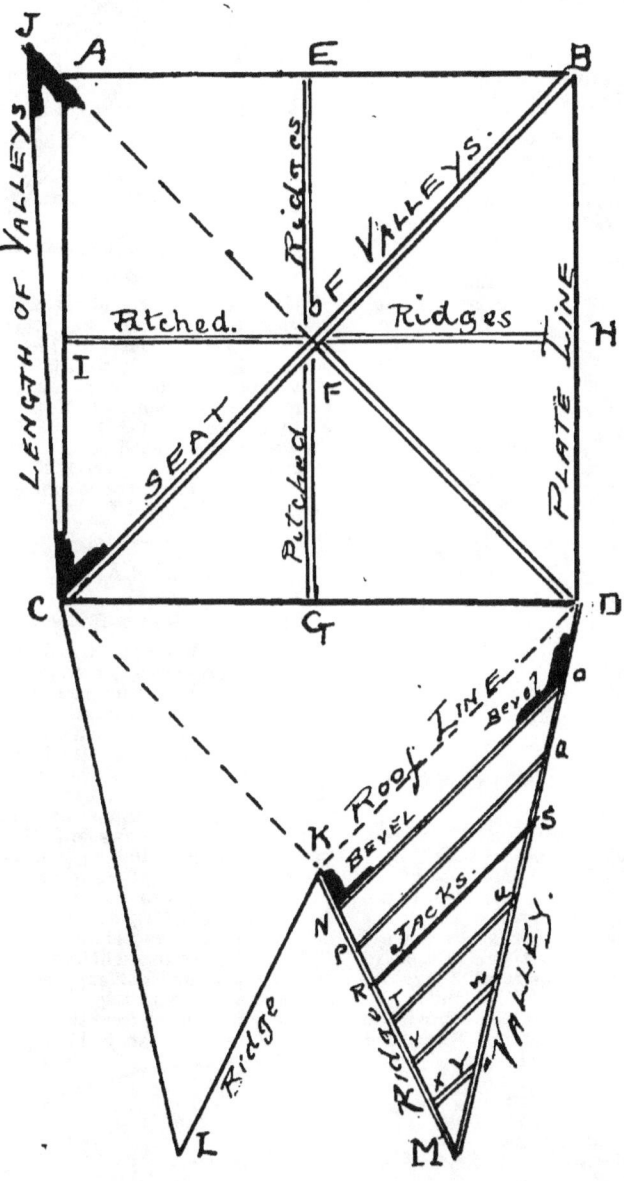

FIG. 72—LAYOUT OF ROOF.

feet higher than the gable peaks so that the ridges rise on pitch in the manner shown in the cross section Fig. 71, thus forming a very peculiar and unusual form of roof.

In order to frame this roof in the simplest manner proceed to Fig. 72, and let A E, B, H, D C, be the plan of the roof A F, B F, D F and C F, being the seats of the valleys. E F, H F, G F, and I F, being the seats or plans of the hips. To find length of valley from F square up as F, A J, equal in height to at C Fig. 71, and join J C, Fig. 72 for the lengths and bevels of the four valley rafters. Now for the eighteen jack rafters the author has found it most convenient to develop the roof in order to prove the accuracy

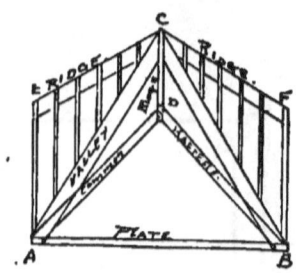

FIG. 71.—VALLEYS, RAFTERS AND RIDGES.

of the methods, or first paste the engraving on cardboard and then cut out as follows:—Cut out the whole plan, A E B H D, M K L C, and A; then make a slight cut with a pocket-knife or chisel from C, to K, and from K, to D, also across C G D. Fold over the development until K, is over G D M, is over D F C L over C F, and L, and M, joined together are over F, with the ridge L K, over G F.

CHAPTER XXVI.

TO FRAME A ROUND-HOUSE ROOF.

ASSUME the roof to be semi circular in plan as represented in Fig. 74, and to have a pitched roof with a ridge, the pitch being half, or 12 and 12 on the steel square, as seen at D, G, F, Fig. 74, where the lengths of the rafters and bevels are delineated. A, B, C and D, E, F, are the gables on the plan Fig. 74 seen on the elevation Fig. 73, with windows and doors in same. In order to find the length of the common rafter simply raise up from E, Fig. 74, the pitch or rise E, G and join D, G. As the outer plate line A, X, F, is much longer than the inner plate line C, Z, D, more rafters will be required so as to form a sufficient support for the roof boards and covering. For this reason an extra rafter from the plate line A, X, F. to the ridge B, K, I, E, must

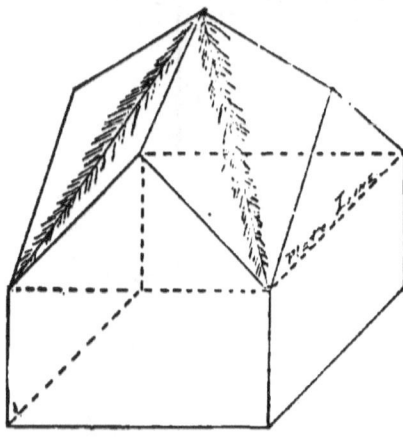

FIG. 70.—GENERAL APPEARANCE OF ROOF.

of the layout; therefore on C G D, erect one gable to stand over C G D, as C K D. From D, make D M, equal in length to F J, and K M, equal in length to the ridge E, C, or C F, Fig. 71. Divide off on K M, Fig. 3, the jack rafters as on K M, Fig. 71, and draw them parallel to K' D, in the way illustrated at Fig. 72, as N O, P Q R S, T U, V W, and X Y. The bevels at O, and N, Fig. 72, will be the side bevels against the ridges and valleys, being reversed for different right and left sides, the down or vertical cut of the bottom ends of the jacks nailed against the valley sides will be as the pitch of the valleys and the top cuts as that of the gables or mitre cut. Carpenters should cut this diagram out, as it is printed, to prove the accuracy

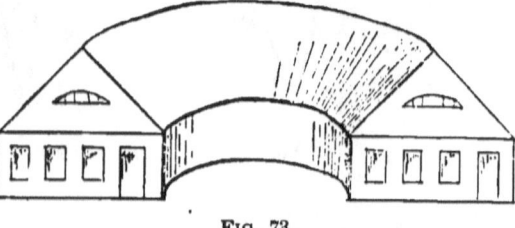

FIG. 73.

be inserted between each abutting rafter so as to equalize the spacing and obtain a stable roof.

The proper way to find the shape of the roof boards is seen at the bottom side of Fig. 74. Divide D, H. into 10 equal parts. or more if desired, then with O, as centre and O. 1, as radius, describe a curve. similarly describe from D. 2. 3, 4. 5, 6. 7, 8, 9 and 10. which will of course bring the boards up to the

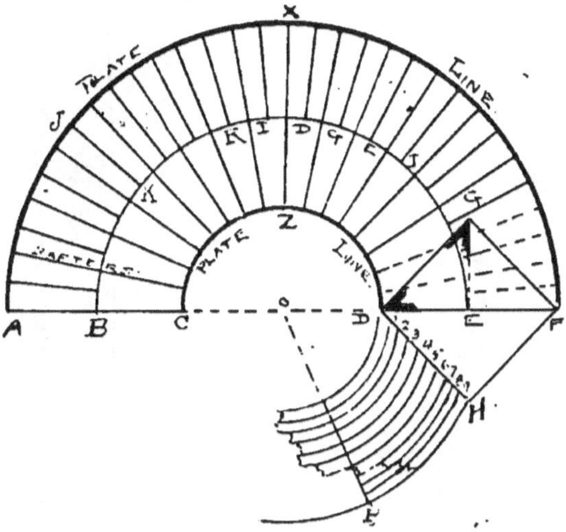

FIG. 74.

ridge line. Now take the distance from E to I and set it off from H to P, the centre of the rafter at I, and this will give the lengths of boards for one section. A like method can be followed for covering the outside slope of the roof. This roof is of a very rare kind and is only found on railroads where locomotives are stored or on large estates for barns or outhouses.

CHAPTER XXVII.

FRAMING A CANTILEVER ROOF.

IN answer to a letter requesting me to illustrate and describe a cantilever roof, I submit for the benefit of all students of carpentry the following design for a roof of this description, which will be adaptable either for a large shed or station.

The engraving, Fig 75, shows a a transverse or cross section of the shed, which may be any length desired, the width (covered) shown is 48' 0", at a sca'e of ¼ inch — 1 foot. If the width

be reduced half, timbers half the width and thickness given here will be sufficient The height to under side of straining beam is 13' 0", to ridge 26' 6". The construction of this building is very simple and is fully illustrated by the drawing. It consists of a series of concrete footings about 3 feet or 4 feet square, placed on sand or hard clay 24' 0" apart. measuring from centre to centre across; and 10' 0" apart, measuring from centre to centre, longitudinally or lengthways. On top of these footings is set a good blue or granite stone mortised out to receive the bottom ends of the posts or uprights. These details constitute the foundation.

The frame superstructure primarily consists of the series of 10"x10" yellow pine square posts, which are tenoned at top and bottom ends. at the bottom to fit into the bottom stone and at the top to receive the 10" x 10" stringer beam or plate A. This longitudinal plate or stringer is mortised to receive the top ends of the posts and the top ends of the diagonal braces H. which stiffen the whole structure lengthways. When constructing this shed the posts, braces and stringers should first be framed, put together. raised and temporarily braced across before commencing to frame the truss roof.

Before commencing the latter a close study should be made of the different constructive details of the roof and the lengths and forms carefully noted and studied out in order not to spoil any of the timber.

The first important detail is the straining beam B This stick should be procured 50' 0" long. laid out and wrought as follows: First, the proper position of the stringers A, 24'0"between centres is laid out on the under side. also laid out and gained for the braces D. Then directly in the centre of this distance on the top side of the beam, position of the king tie C, is laid off and distinctly marked. Directly over the position of the stringers a mortise to receive the short 6" x 10" posts F is made on both ends. also the opposite ends are notched or gained out for the feet of the principal rafters E, in the manner shown, about 2" down in the beam.

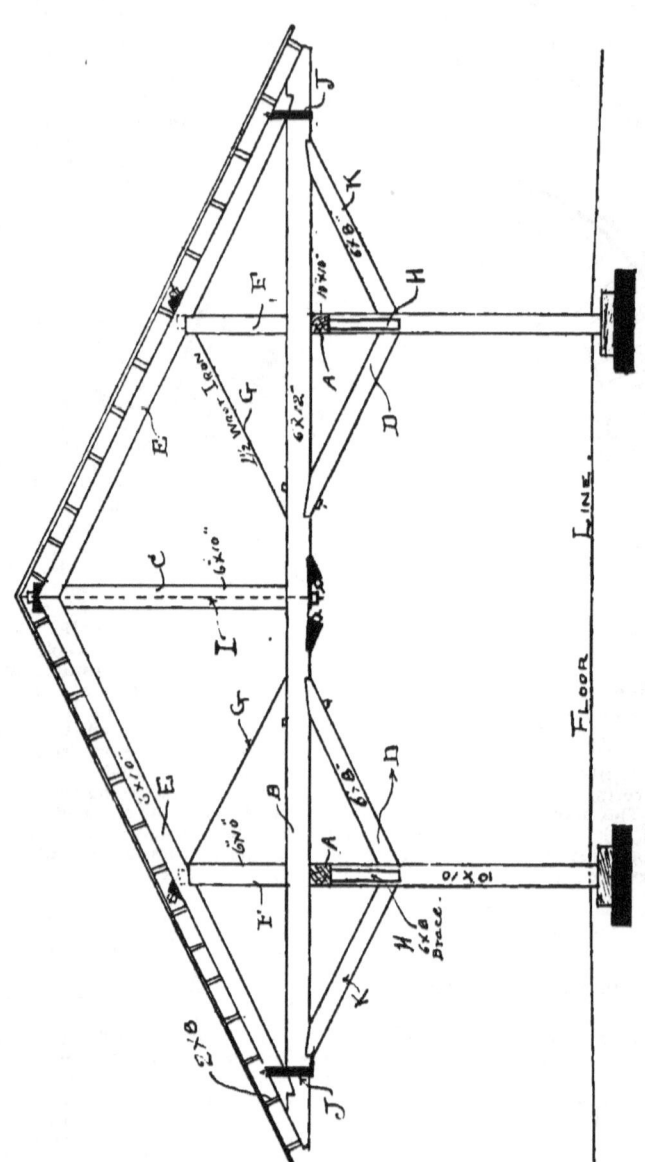

FIG. 75—DESIGN AND DETAILS OF CANTILEVER ROOF. SCALE $\frac{1}{4}''$ = 1 FOOT.

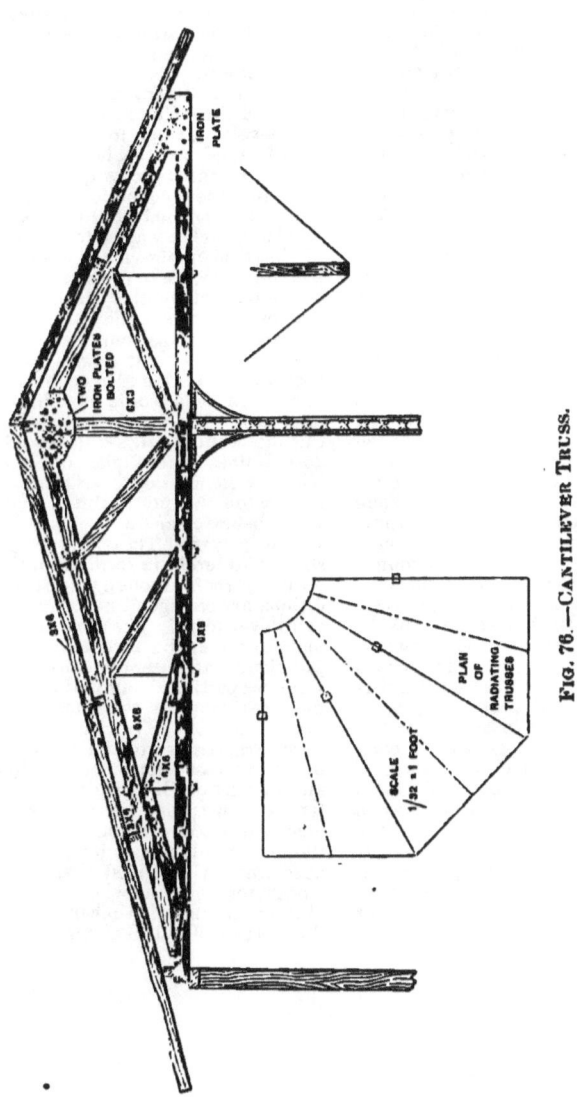

FIG. 76.—CANTILEVER TRUSS.

Next the *principal rafters* G, are mortised out for the short posts, cut to the exact length as given, to the top bevel and notch required to fit into the straining beam. It is also bored out for the wrought iron rods and bolts G. delineated. The *straining beams* are likewise bored for these irons. The *short posts* F, and *braces* D are finally framed with the usual *tenons* and the *truss* is ready to be put together.

In doing this the proper way to proceed is to first set the straining beam B. then to insert the tenons of the *short posts* F, into their mortises. next the *king tie* C, and finally the principal rafters E. The vertical bolts I, and washers are next inserted and the straps J put on. This operation must of course be gone through on each *truss*, and the whole number finished before commencing to raise them into their permanent position on top of the stringer beams AA. The raising can be done with a good gin pole or derrick. When the trusses are set vertically on stringers AA, to form the appearance seen in the engraving, directly over the posts below, each one should be well braced with 2" x 4" joists to prevent it from being blown or knocked down. Each truss should also be set perfectly plumb sideways. If desired, the outer braces KK may be omitted and the wrought iron rod G inserted to counterbalance the overhanging portion of the roof. The space inside the braces may also be filled in with ornamental scroll work. either in iron or wood. In regard to the strains on the different timbers I would say that the *straining beam* B is in tension. the *braces* K and D underneath to the posts are in compression. The *principal rafters* are in compression. The *king tie* C is in compression and the *purlins* bear a lateral strain across the fibres. The bolts are wrought iron. The washers and plates cast iron *Straps* are of wrought iron ¼" x 2". This roof may be safely covered with shingles, or metal shingles, or tar paper.

It will be noticed that I have given in this description a full written and detailed description of the construction of this roof and "mode of procedure" necessary to be followed in building it. The years which I have studied construction have taught me that much detailed information is never superfluous in conveying accurate mechanical practice to others.

The truss illustrated at Fig. 76 was designed by Walter P. Rice, C. E., of Cleveland, Ohio, for the roof of the grand stand at the baseball park in that city, and reflects great credit on him for the economical manner in which he disposed of the constructive details in such a way as to leave a view of the field unobstructed. As will be seen on reference to the plan the portion of the roof where the cantilevers were employed covered the portion on the corners which was contained in the two sides placed at right angles, and had a post been placed under each truss the view of the field would have been much intercepted To avoid this he suspended. the intervening trusses shown by the dotted lines on the plan on iron rods which were carried over those trusses resting on the posts, thus leaving the space below clear for the spectators to see the players. These trusses are but slightly different in form from those in ordinary roofs, though the static conditions are changed on account of the cantilever form. The drawing will explain to readers its form and show how judiciously and economically the pieces were proportioned, also how the engineer, realizing by calculation that the greater part of the vertical strain would necessarily be exerted on the front columns, increased its efficiency by using an iron post of the diagonal lattice pattern of the proportions shown. The idea is an excellent one and worthy of the high reputation of its designer. It need scarcely be added that the entire workmanship of the whole construction of the stand. mostly timber, was done in the most creditable manner.

www.ingramcontent.com/pod-product-compliance
Lightning Source LLC
Chambersburg PA
CBHW021234260626
47172CB00002B/755

* 9 7 8 3 3 3 7 3 8 7 3 0 3 *